KANIKSU TWO

Masselow, Fabled Waters, She Who Sees and Other Stories

BY

THOMAS F. LACY

ISBN: 1-4107-6571-7 (e-book)
ISBN: 1-4107-6570-9 (Paperback)

This book is printed on acid free paper.

1stBooks – rev. 08/08/03

For Franny

Cover Painting, Hunt Lake
By
Leo Desimpel

FORWARD

They call it the Idaho Panhandle National Forest now. There isn't much romance in the name. But the name of the three national forests it supplanted had plenty of romance. The Coeur d'Alene. The St. Joe. The Kaniksu. Kaniksu is an Indian word meaning "black robe" and is thought to be the original name of Priest Lake. Although our families had been neighbors at Priest Lake since 1922, it wasn't until 1989 that I met Tom Lacy. He had heard (erroneously) that I was a decent fisherman and tracked me down at the cabin, where I was bedridden with several broken ribs. During that initial meeting, Tom informed me that he wasn't a lake fisherman and would like me to accompany him to the streams he had fished as a boy. About a month later, the doctor gave me the go ahead to start doing some walking and Tom figured that meant hiking all over hell and gone. I could barely walk upright, using my rod case for a cane, he had a history of mini-strokes. It was an adventure.

Over the next few years we fished Tom's fishing holes and the fishing was great. It was the catching that wasn't very good. We also picked a few huckleberries, took some hikes, and generally gallivanted around the lake. Tom provided me with a window to the past and I was hoping to capture his memories on videotape. But Tom said, "That's what the book is for", and he published KANIKSU Stories of the Northwest in 1994. It is a

v

collection of stories about people Tom encountered during the 20's and 30's in northern Idaho and western Montana. Now Tom has written the sequel, KANIKSU TWO a further collection of stories including his father's memoirs, the stage holdup, and the story of the Kalispell Indian people. Like his first book, it is written with Tom's gentle sense of humor and it opens that window to the past in the Kaniksu.

Your Pal,

Mr. Luby

ACKNOWLEDGEMENTS

I would like to thank those whose assistance and support have helped me produce Kaniksu Two. My computer early on evidenced a mind of its own and only with the help of Kit Simmons did it perform. It will give me great pleasure to relegate it to duty as a boat anchor.

Though Jim Luby does occasionally stoop to fishing for Macs, I do highly recommend him as a fishing partner and friend. I thank him profusely for the rare photo of Old Man Williamson and for his fine Forward.

Alice Ignace O'Connor, Kalispel elder and friend, provided the Kalispel Legends and much background information and inspiration for the Masselow and She Who Sees stories. She taught me how to play the Stick Game. Thanks Alice.

Lois Hill is a longtime friend and mushroom picking partner. I owe her many thanks for editing and help with the mushroom story.

Thomas Hunter, friend, fishing partner and also ex ad man read the first drafts and offered invaluable support and suggestions. Tom is a fine artist and writer and should combine these talents in producing a book.

Jeanne Tomlin, granddaughter of Charles Beardmore, provided the stage coach picture and background information on Charles for the stage coach hold up story. Thank you very much Jeanne.

Daniel Matson, archeologist, provided background data and counsel when I was in the research stage of the project. Many thanks Daniel.

Charlotte Jones, granddaughter of Leonard Paul who produced the postcards of the steamer, Jack Pine Flats, etc., approved my use of them in Kaniksu Two. Thanks Charlotte.

Michelle Graye and Daniel Simmons, librarians, helped me with library matters. Thank you both very much.

And to Daisy Njoku and the Smithsonian, many thanks for the use of the picture of Masselow. It is a wonderful Edward Curtis picture, and I am so grateful to have it in the book.

John R. Fahey, Professor Emeritus Eastern Washington University and author, many thanks for editing and counsel with Masselow story.

Many thanks to all.

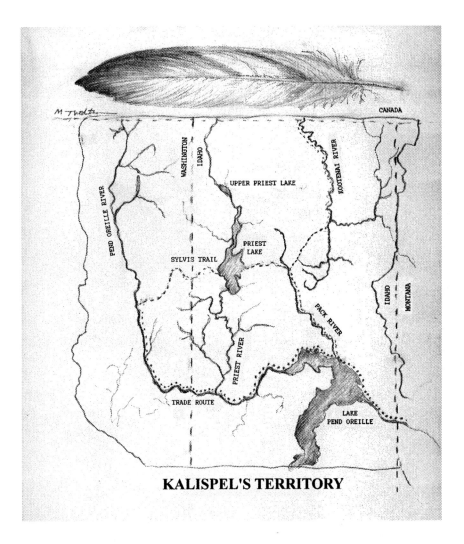

KALISPEL'S TERRITORY

The lands of the Kalispel were laced with trails, the most important being the Sylvis Trail and the Trade Route. The Sylvis Trail gave the Kalispel access to the bountiful hunting and fishing around Priest Lake, and the Trade Route access to the buffalo hunting in Montana. That section of the Sylvis Trail, from the Indian Campgrounds at the north end of Luby Bay to the West Branch Road, was still in use in the twenties. We often hiked over it to the West Branch Road, south on it to the Sherman Trail, returning on the Sherman Trail to Luby Bay.

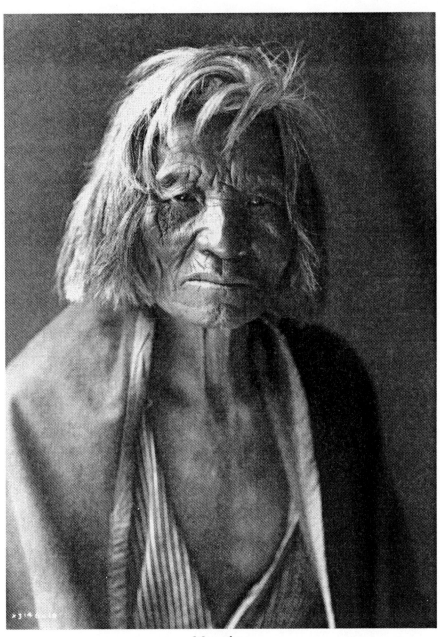

Masselow
Photographed c. 1910 by Edward S. Curtis
National Anthropological Archives,
Smithsonian Institution / 83-14079

Chapter 1

Indian Painted Rock, Calispell Bay, Priest Lake, Idaho.

MASSELOW

Masselow poured a little flour into the ancient blue chipped enamel bowl. He added warm water, let it thicken, and then downed a few spoonfuls. He took a sip of tea from a matching blue enameled cup.

It could have been breakfast, lunch, or dinner for he had no way of tracing the path of the sun and telling the time of day. He was blind from a lifetime of exposure to the smoky interior of a tepee.

Masselow and his people, the remnant left, were brought to the edge of starvation by the policies of the United States Government. For over six decades the government tried to get the Kalispel to "remove" from their ancestral lands along the ntxwe River (Pend Oreille). They were told, "The Great Father in Washington wishes you to release any claims you have to the land and "remove" to the Colville, the Coeur 'd Alene, or the Flathead Reservation."

"Remove"...an innocent enough word...but when hung over you for six decades and means giving up your homelands, lands you roamed freely over, lands that hold the spirits of your ancestors, lands you love, it becomes a crushing, grinding torture that would destroy most people.

Masselow and his people politely declined to "remove". One hundred people against the overwhelming power of the United States government, they would never give in, never give up.

It was not always that way. In the world that Masselow came into on April 20, 1826, food was bountiful and life idyllic. The lands of the Kalispel swept across what is now northeastern Washington, northern Idaho, and into Montana, over three million acres of dark green forests, spectacular granite tipped mountain peaks, deep blue lakes, and pure clear rivers and streams.

These were the good years, the happy years, the romantic years. The living was peaceful, simple. Few whites had intruded on their lands and only briefly; Lewis and Clark in 1804 and David Thompson and Alexander Henry of the North West Company, fur traders, in 1809 and 1810.

Their main village was on a widening of the ntxwe River nine miles downriver from present day Newport. The village lay on a low bank on the east side of the river. The romantic white bleached tepees and green tule mat covered long lodges reached downriver as far as the eye could see. In the evenings with fires lit within, the tepees appeared like lighted lanterns. Over to the west lay great fields of grass and camas that turned a shimmering lavender in early summer. The whole was enclosed with dark green pine clad mountains.

Masselow had come into a people who treasured their independence and lived as a large family, a family a few years earlier said to have over 1500 members. Theirs was a society with common ownership of property. There were three main bands each with a chief and sub-chief and a central tribal authority or chief, at this time, Standing Grizzly, grandfather of Masselow. It was he who parceled out the hunting, fishing and gathering areas, divided the stores of meat, fish, camas and berries. He judged disputes and meted out punishments, the most serious being whippings.

It was a wonderful time in the life of Masselow. He was witness to the Kaniksu in its natural state; the great numbers of deer, caribou, elk, mountain goats, buffalo, and bear, the great spawning runs of cutthroat trout, whitefish, and salmon that filled the streams from bank to bank. Masselow saw the pristine forests untouched by saw or axe. He drank from the pure clean rivers, streams, and lakes. Only the trails and tepees betrayed the presence of the Kalispel.

The Kalispel had many horses that had come up the trade routes from the southwest. Every boy was given a horse at an early age. So

2

Masselow had a horse of his own to range freely over the many trails that laced their vast lands. He and the other boys would ride herd on the Kalispel horses to keep other Indians from stealing them, a common sport among tribes.

The Kalispel lands were interwoven with trails. Masselow could put a few dried camas and dried venison in a leather pouch and take off on one of these trails. He could cover fifty to a hundred miles in a day on horse, enough to reach Chal Qe Lee (Priest Lake), Kettle Falls, or Pend Oreille Lake.

The Kalispel had a unique canoe, really more kayak than canoe. The frame was made of pine and cedar, covered with inner bark of pine, and was only a couple of hands deep. The fore and aft sloped to the water and they, too, were covered with inner bark of pine providing dry storage. The design gave it greater maneuverability and safety in high winds and rough water. It took a week to build one. Every family had one or more. Masselow would have had one to fish and explore the ntxwe and its tributaries.

The Kalispel had a freedom few other people have known. They were independent, self sufficient, nomadic by nature. In the spring of the year when stores of food were low, they broke up into small bands and spread out through their vast lands to hunt, and fish, and gather roots and berries.

They trailed poles and tule mats, which they used to build temporary shelters wherever they stopped. Chal Qe Le with its abundant deer, caribou, bear, mountain goat, small animals and great runs of whitefish and trout was a favored spot. Most bands returned to the villages on the ntxwe for the camas digging and festivities.

Kalispel legend tells that it was Frog who led them to the camas beds. "Long ago when the people and animals spoke to each other and the Kalispel lived on the shores of Chal Qe Le, Frog one day decided to climb the highest mountain to the west and see what lay on the other side. From there he saw a large lavender lake shimmering in the distance. He hurriedly returned to tell his friends, the Kalispel, of his wondrous discovery. A scouting party was sent out to investigate and discovered that it was not a lake but vast beds of lavender flowers of the camas waving in the breeze."

This was a peaceful time, the living simple unhurried. The Kalispel and their neighbors, the Spokanes, the Colvilles, the Coeur d' Alenes, the Flatheads lived together harmoniously. They all spoke the Salishan language indicating a common origin. These other tribes visited the Kalispel in early summer to harvest their winter supply of camas. It was a festival, a social gathering, a celebration, a most exciting time.

The camas digging as with most food gathering was preceded with prayers. Then the women pried the camas bulbs from the moist soil with sharp sticks. They were then steamed in rock-lined pit-ovens for several days, dried in the sun and bagged. Others were ground in stone mortars, baked with black moss, formed into black cakes and stored. Still others were pulled steaming from the ovens, coated with bear grease or deer marrow and eaten. Some were dried and stored, lasting for years. It was said, "Three dried camas a day could keep a man alive a year."

The men raced their horses and threw stakes at rolling hoops. There were diving and wrestling contests for young men. Young men and women competed against each other in hopping and running contests. Men and women played a shinny-like game with a stuffed buckskin ball. The most exciting game was the stick game pitting Kalispel teams against the visitors. It was accompanied with heavy betting.

In the evenings, there was dancing around great bonfires that often ran into the early morning hours. Inter-tribal marriages often resulted from these festivals.

In return, the Colville and Spokane Indians invited the Kalispel to fish for salmon ascending their rivers. Salmon did not ascend the ntxwe. Kalispel legend explained that it was because of coyote that long ago came to them looking for a wife, and they turned him down. Coyote uprooted the ntxwe forming a waterfall that blocked the passage of the salmon.

The Colvilles controlled the salmon fishing at Kettle Falls. It was dangerous exciting. The fishermen balanced on great boulders or wooden stands built out over the river and speared or netted the salmon as they leaped out of the roiling water. They also speared the salmon at night by firelight.

The Kalispel gathered bitterroot on the lands of the Coeur d' Alene and hunted buffalo on Blackfoot lands. In the fall, they shot large quantities of deer, elk, caribou, mountain goat, bear and dried it for later consumption.

When snow started moving down the mountainsides, the band returned to their villages along the ntxwe and their tepees and lodges. The lodges were typically twelve feet wide and fifty feet long depending on the number of families living in them. They were basically a pole A-frame covered with tule mats.

Snow lay heavy on the land in those days, sometime as much as twelve feet. It was a time for the women to repair clothing and sew new moccasins, leggings, ponchos and dresses, and men to repair tools, chip arrowheads and hunt in the nearby hills. Girls worked with their mothers and boys with their fathers to learn the arts, crafts, and culture of the Kalispel.

4

With two or three families living together, it was confining. To break the monotony they played games; children spun tops and adults threw beaver tooth dice and played the stick game. Storytellers told stories handed down from generation to generation around the fires in the evening. But it was the medicine dances, often lasting several weeks, which did the most to relieve the winter monotony.

A special shelter was built that had the capacity of four or five lodges with open top. Three fires were made in the center, and the rest of the floor was covered with soft pine branches upon which buffalo skins were spread forming the dance floor. Though the temperature would drop to twenty degrees below zero the dancers would be dressed only at the waist, the rest painted red or red striped.

The dancers were so close together that they stood with arms raised, thumbs touching shoulders and the only movement that of the upper body up and down. The dancing was accompanied with medicine songs and the recounting of stories of valor. These dances often lasted several weeks. The dancers went from tribe to tribe to participate in them.

Hunting was carried out throughout the year. Shortly after the winter medicine dance entire villages would go into the low mountains to hunt for deer. Deep snows higher up brought deer down where forage was more readily available. Here the Kalispel would conduct drives and force the deer into drifts where they were dispatched with clubs and arrows.

The Kalispel ways and customs were about to change. Since time immemorial Kalispel boys on reaching puberty had gone on a Vision Quest to seek a Guardian Spirit and a vision of what life held in store for them. Masselow in 1839 was probably one of the last boys to go on Vision Quest. Rumors were already circulating of men in black robes who had come into the fringes of their land bringing a new religion more powerful than any before.

"The Black Robes"

Black Robes was the Kalispel word for the Jesuit priests, a fitting word that quickly brings to mind an image of these remarkable men, who more than any other men influenced the ways of the Kalispel. Foreseeing the devastating effects of the growing numbers of whites pouring into the west they attempted to change the Kalispel from hunter-gatherers to cattlemen farmers.

Father Pierre Jean De Smet was the first Catholic priest to visit them. In November 1841 barely ahead of the winter freeze, he made an epic dash from Saint Mary's Mission in Montana to Fort Colville in Washington. He traveled down the trade route along the Pend Oreille River finally coming upon the main Kalispel village on a wide expanse of the river. Here the valley spread out in a broad lush grassy plain. The Kalispel and Standing Grizzly had been waiting eagerly for their coming and rushed out to greet them. They had been foretold that men in Black Robes were coming to tell them of a powerful religion.

Father De Smet baptized 140 of the Kalispels including Standing Grizzly who took the name of Loyola. It was the beginning of a six-year relationship that grew in mutual esteem and affection.

Despite being a Superior in the Catholic Church for that region Father De Smet did make a number of visits over the years to the Kalispels. The first Christmas he celebrated Mass with them in a picturesque cave on a hillside nearby. He was so taken with its natural beauty he named it New Manresa Grotto after a similar grotto in Europe.

He assigned Father Hoecken. a Dutch priest, and brother McGean to found a mission. A mission was hastily erected on land that unfortunately overflowed in high water. De Smet returned and picked out a site on higher ground near New Manresa Groto. Here the Kalispel built a church of dressed logs, a priest's house, stable, barn, shop and a gristmill. They also erected several log cabins. They named the mission St. Ignatius. The mission lent stability to the Kalispel and a center of activity.

De Smet returned in the spring with plows, axes, spades, scythes, and carpenters for a permanent settlement and farming. They planted 160 acres, but the first crops were poor. But as time passed they broke ground on more fertile ground and put 300 acres to growing wheat, potatoes, barley, onions, cabbage, parsnips, peas, beets and carrots.

Standing Grizzly gave up hunting and devoted his days to Father Hoecken and an interpreter learning the Catholic religion. In the evenings he taught tribal headmen lessons he had learned during the day. Most members embraced Catholic teachings, but there were a few who still preferred the buffalo hunting, the chase, gambling, shamans, fetishes and talismans.

DeVos, now taking over from Father De Smet as Superior, approached Loyola on moving to ground more suitable to farming with another tribe. Loyola spoke with his people, but they were divided on the proposal. Loyola made the decision for them to stay. Loyola died April 6, 1846 and was succeeded by a son, Victor, whom the priests thought weak but held steadfastly for a reservation on Kalispel land.

"Remove"

The next sixty years saw the freest people on earth losing their freedom, their millions of acres of homelands reduced to just a few, the abundant supply of fish, game, and root crops dwindle, the remnant of their people brought to the edge of starvation, their virgin forests raped, their choicest bottom lands fenced and cultivated, their leader falsely accused of crimes he did not commit and jailed, roads laid over their trails, steamers plying and polluting their navigable waters where once only their quiet picturesque canoes plied the waters, Priest Lake and Pend Oreille Lake ringed with mines and the tailings run out into the waters. And the pressures grew for them to "remove" to a far off reservation.

1853 Isaac Stevens former major in the army engineers was named the first governor of Washington Territory. He was committed by federal fiat to persuade the Indians to cede their lands and "remove" to a reservation. He was also committed to scout for a northern route for a railroad, a railroad that undoubtedly would bring hordes of settlers and commerce into the area. An unseen noose had slipped over the heads of the Kalispel.

In a spring meeting in 1856, R.H. Lansdale, a member of Stevens' Indian Service, met with the Kalispel and outlined a treaty with them. For ceding their lands, the Kalispel would receive $40,000 over twenty years, a grist mill, saw mill, hospital and physician, agricultural- industrial school with teachers, and various shops with men to work in them and teach the Kalispel to be carpenters, blacksmiths, or gun, wagon, or plow makers.

The Kalispel would be united with the Flathead on the Flathead reservation. Victor countered, offering half their land south and west of the Pend Oreille River. The Kalispel would keep the half north and east of the river. This Lansdale said he could not do. The next day Victor said the Kalispel had decided not to sell without a reservation on their own lands.

Plots of uprising and war circulated throughout the territory. Sub Chief of the Spokane Indians, Polatkin and Kamiakin of the Yakima plotted to form a defense coalition to drive out the whites. Most of the Kalispels declined to join although a few of their young hot blood braves did. Liquor fanned the flames of hatred. In mid 1857 Stevens was elected a delegate to congress.

Finally with rumors of Indian plots growing and Palouse Indian raids on settler's cattle, Colonel Steptoe of the Walla Walla army post moved out with 150 poorly armed and trained men in an attempt to quell the Indians. Near Rosalia he was attacked by the coalition and driven back to a hillock. He was surrounded, but under cover of darkness he and his men escaped to Walla Walla.

In retaliation, the army assembled a force of trained soldiers from other posts and sent them north from WallaWalla under Major George Wright. Wright's artillery, infantry and dragoon juggernaut met the coalition southwest of Spokane Falls. Wright moved his infantry forward. He then sent his dragoons, sabers slashing among the Indians, killing twenty and wounding fifty. The Indians had never encountered such overwhelming force and fled.

Four days later he found the Indians drawn up on rocky terrain where his dragoons could not be used so effectively. The Indians had set fire to the grasses sending smoke billowing over Wright's forces. Yet Wright was able to drive the Indians back.

He pursued the Indians to the Coeur d'Alene mission where they surrendered, granting hostages but no culprits. October 1858 General Harney proclaimed peace in the interior northwest.

In 1862 congress passed the Homestead Act and in 1863 formed the Idaho Territory. The 1864 congress chartered the Northern Pacific Railroad to follow the route surveyed by Stevens to be subsidized with alternate grants of land. Stevens County was created by the legislature to serve the area from the Cascades to the Bitterroots.

Large numbers of displaced Indians roamed through what was left of open land trying to maintain the nomadic life, hunting, fishing, and gathering. Pinkney City, which sprang up during the gold mining days, had become a town of corruption, populated with desperados driven out of southern Idaho towns, drunken Indians, prostitute Indian women. It had six licensed saloons. Victor complained that traders were bringing whiskey onto Kalispel lands and selling it to Indians.

Over the next few years a series of plans were advanced by agents to provide the Indians with lands and a treaty; the Winans Plan, the Yantis Plan, the Shanks Plan advanced a series of plans, but in general congress failed to act on them. The interior boiled in uncertainty and bitterness. Lands for hunting and fishing were diminishing. An aging shaman was preaching to Indians that Indian dead would rise up to drive out the whites, stirring some of the camps.

The Northern Pacific Railroad reached Spokane Falls in July of 1881 and eastern and western tracks were joined in September 1883 at Gold Creek, Montana. With the conclusion of the Northern Pacific and the advertising for settlers, there came an inflow of farmers, miners, and loggers into Kalispel territory. The Kalispel tried to keep them out, but their lands kept shrinking with industry and settlers. The Kalispel homelands now held logging mills, mines, railroads, and towns where once there were only trading posts. The noose had tightened.

The Kalispel were vilified and reviled. They were accused of murdering white prospectors in their mountains, accusations that were never proved. Settlers accused the Kalispel of stealing from them. Masselow was arrested on a burglary charge so flimsy the judge threw it out of court and released him. It was a difficult time for the Kalispel, yet they accepted the inhumanity without rancor, the intolerance with tolerance, the indignity with dignity, and the greed with generosity.

The government's policy at this time was to consolidate tribes and reduce the number of reservations. To carry out this policy congress formed the Northwest Indian Commission in 1886. Three men were sent by the U.S. Government to meet with the Kalispel to sign a treaty, Judge John V. Wright chairman, Jarred W. Daniels and Henry W. Andrews. They arrived in Spokane February 1887. They set up a meeting in Sandpoint. The commissioners had heard Masselow, who had recently been made chief of the Kalispel, was obstinate, untamed, and contrary.

Judge Wright opened the meeting saying, "My friends we have been sent by authority of the United States Government to meet with you and discuss your present condition and future welfare."

"The white man is coming onto your land and disturbing you and because you are located where you are we will not be able to protect you from them. The government wishes you to release any claims you have to the land and "remove" to the Colville, Coeur d'Alene or Flathead reservations."

"You will receive a home for every family. The head of each family shall receive 160 acres, each person over 18 shall receive 80 acres, 40 acres for those under 18, and 80 acres for each orphan child. You will receive horses, cows, assistance in plowing and fencing the fields, men to teach you milling, carpentry, smithing and other skills, a sawmill and a gristmill. Victor is growing old. He shall have $100 per year as long as he lives. The Great Father in Washington wants this treaty and if he didn't care for you would not have sent us. I hope you will open your hearts and not refuse his hand when he offers it to you."

It was the same flowery speech and promises they had heard before. Masselow replied. "It would be a crime if we have to give up the land given us by the Great Spirit. You say we will be happy. We will not be happy until we die. We wish to talk together, and we will talk to you again tomorrow at noon."

They met again and the Kalispel asked for a piece of their land to live on and give the rest to the Great Chief in Washington. The commissioners said they could not do this and they must go to another reservation.

The Pend Oreille Kalispel agreed to a treaty and moved to the Jocko Reservation in Montana, but never received the benefits promised. Masselow and Victor refused to sign the treaty and returned to their village.

By 1890, the Pend Oreille valley was being settled rapidly by homesteaders, farmers and cattlemen. In 1891-92, the land office issued homestead patents for 8280 acres of Kalispel homelands. Steamers ran between Newport and points downward. The Kalispel made a little money peddling huckleberries, venison and beadwork, supplemented with hunting, fishing and their garden.

Building of the Great Northern was bringing waves of settlers, speculators and a rough element working on the railroad. Pressure and intimidation was building up on the Kalispel to sell their lands. Masselow and several Kalispel road on horscback to Colville seeking help from Captain John W. Bubb acting agent in getting relief from whites who were trying to freeze them out and falsely accusing them of stealing from them.

Victor in his last hours called the tribe together and urged them to remain on the east side of the river and be buried there. This was in 1891. A Priest River Reserve was established in 1898 closing thousands of acres of Kalispel lands to their use. The noose drew tight,

The commissioner in Washington instructed Bubb to survey all of Kalispel lands; three claims on the west side of the river and the remainder on the east side. He stated that those who would swindle them are willing to attribute all kinds of misdemeanors to them and deny them peaceful residence in the valley.

Logging companies had moved in from Michigan, Minnesota, and Pennsylvania and were logging along the banks of the Pend Oreille. Poles were being barged upriver to Newport and cut into lumber there for homes or shipped east on the Northern Pacific or Great Northern. Diamond Match and Dalkena Lumber Companies were logging over at Priest Lake, floating the logs down to the lake in log flumes, gathering them in log booms and in the spring of the year driving them down to Priest River to be cut into lumber at the mills there. Priest River was becoming a bustling boomtown.

At this time a number of silver, lead and zinc mines sprang up around Priest Lake; The Gem Mining Co., Pan Handle, Cabinet, Range, Kutenai, Pack, and the Continental up near the Canadian border. In 1904 Leonard Paul opened a store at the south end of the lake to supply the miners, loggers, homesteaders, and the Forest Service. He also traded with the Kalispel Indians who came over to net white fish at Soldier and Kalispel Creeks; food for skins and moccasins. At this time the W.W. Slee launch operated on Priest Lake transporting supplies and people. The Kalispel were pretty much shut out of their lands and facing starvation. Masselow was now blind.

The Indian office in Washington was considering drafting a presidential order designating a Kalispel reservation but decided individual allotments under the Dawes act of 1887 would be better. There was a problem with allotments, Federal Law called for 160 acres for each head of household and 80 acres for a single person. Only enough land remained to allot 40 acres of farmland and 80 acres of grazing land. Another problem with allotments was the Kalispel had always occupied their land in common.

Late in June 1911 Masselow now blind and feeble was to make one final effort to obtain a homeland for his people. He traveled sixty miles to Gonzaga College in Spokane to solicit the help of the Jesuit Fathers. He called on Father Louis Taelman, president of Gonzaga. He described the condition of his people, and pleaded for help in obtaining a church, a school, and a reservation for his people. Since the time of De Smet the Kalispel had been devout Catholic. It was twenty-five years since they had been visited by a priest and mass said in the Kalispel village.

Father Taelman was touched and visited the Kalispel village. He found them destitute and facing starvation. He visited them often over the next two years. He conducted mass, and his trips were widely reported in the newspapers. He launched a campaign to bring a school to the Kalispel children. He brought the plight of the Kalispel to the attention of influential people in Washington. His efforts got results. Congressman W. La Follette entered an amendment to the 1913 Indian Bill providing for a school for the Kalispel and setting aside 4,449 acres for the Kalispel. The amendment was disallowed. But Secretary F.J. Lane drafted an executive order setting aside a reservation of 4600 acres on the east side of the Pend Oreille River in the heart of the Kalispel homeland. President Woodrow Wilson signed the order in 1914.

In his time, Masselow was called obstinate, untamed, and contrary by his enemies. What he was, was resolute. Struck blind, lesser men would have given up. He never gave in. He never gave up. His life is an inspiration to all. He was one of our finest.

Masselow died in 1920, the year congress made education compulsory for all Indian children.

Chapter 2

Trout Fishing, Granite Creek, Priest Lake, Idaho.

THE FABLED WATERS

Like a number of things two fishing partners come to share, fabled waters became a term that indicated special places where trout could be found in numbers. After a while it came to signify wild waters where you expected to catch trout easily and were humbled by their refusals. Fabled waters were places in the mind where everything would come out all right and fishing would seem a reasonable way to spend time. In the end, it was all the intangible qualities of sport shared by two men.

It was Jim who first called some of the waters in the Kaniksu fabled waters.

"You pronounce it fabled as in table," I corrected him.

"No, no. Fabled as in fabulous," he insisted. "Fat fabulous eastern brook trout."

I replied, "Whatever."

Our fishing partnership had started one day in late June. Jim's mother, Dorothy Luby (Saint Dorothy-she had two sons), had stopped me on the path that runs along the shore of Luby Bay on Priest Lake and said that she was concerned about her son Jim's progress following the auto accident, an accident that had splintered five ribs and left him in serious pain, depressed and angry.

"Perhaps a little bit of fishing talk would help lift his spirits," she said to me. "Do you suppose you could find the time to stop by and talk to him?"

"I'll stop by soon," I promised.

Looking back now, I have the feeling that Saint Dorothy, bless her soul, with a woman's intuition and eyes that see into a man's heart, had brought us together as much for my healing as Jim's. Having lost my wife earlier in the year to cancer, and subsequently being hospitalized with a stroke, I was weak, depressed. The cancer is a cruel thing that takes the one and leaves the other half a person. I was angry that it had to be her. She was five years younger than I, and I had always thought she would get to live longer than I.

Before seeing Jim, I inquired around to get a better notion of him. Our paths had never crossed. He was just forty, and I was much older. He had never married. He had an Irishman's reticence towards tying one's self down. His father had not married until he was thirty- nine. But Jim had a sweet girl, Shirley, who gave his mother hope.

I learned Jim's accident occurred on the county road, the highway into the Kaniksu. The driver of the oncoming car had indicated a right turn, then suddenly turned his wheels left, and a loaded pickup truck rear-ended his car throwing it into Jim's light foreign model. Five ribs on Jim's left side were splintered. When I came into his room that first time, the room as dark as his spirits. he lay propped up in his bed. At the foot of his bed in a straight back chair, sat a bushy bearded fellow. "Hap this is the fellow I've been telling you about. Knows where all the big fish are. We'll have great fishing this summer," he said grinning at Hap. Then turning to me, "Hap works for the Forest Service. He fights forest fires. Runs fire fighting crews. He also fishes."

I now noticed that Hap wore the yellow fire retardant shirt with U.S.F.S. stenciled across the front of it.

"How has your fishing been," Hap asked? He had a woodsman's soft voice and a slow easy manner.

"Most of the beaver dams I used to fish are dry and the streams I fished are closed," I replied.

"Closed, to try and restore the cutthroat trout fishery in the lake," Jim put in. "The big macs, stocked in the lake years ago, have pretty much decimated the native cutthroat, dolly varden, and white fish."

"Right," I said. "I did take two brookies from Huff Lake last night. They were so black you couldn't see the mottling on their backs. I've never seen anything like it. Must be that the vegetation growing out over the water decomposes and stains the water which in turn darkens the trout. It is a dying lake." Then half to myself, "The place looks like it should have a resident moose."

This was the first of many visits I was to make over the next few weeks. I always stopped after a fishing expedition to fill him in. There were some minor successes during his recovery. A few west slope cutthroat from Petite Lake and Muskegon Lake. I fished Huff Lake again but caught just one small brookie.

We took to poring over maps, planning what streams and mountain lakes we would fish when Jim was better. One day he pointed to a small creek starting just east of the county road and emptying into Priest Lake at Kalispel Bay.

"Reynolds Creek," he exclaimed. "A friend once confided over a few Hales Ales at Hill's that a beaver dam at the headwaters contains sizable brookies."

"See the two track that runs along the upper end," I pointed out. "We ought to drive up there."

By then Jim was able to ride in a car, so we checked it out. But we could not find a beaver dam and gave it up. We later learned from Austin Raine, a local rancher, that upper Reynolds Creek had been ditched and diverted, its waters eventually emptying into Lamb Creek.

"The beaver dam you are looking for lies to the west of the county road," he told us. He also gave us directions on how to reach it.

I exclaimed in rising excitement, "Any beaver dam that is so well hidden has to have large trout."

And Jim had murmured, "Fabled waters."

By the end of June, Jim was becoming more active. You could see the pain on his face when he caught his foot on a rug or he tried to lower himself into a chair. Then one morning when I was down on the beach reading the morning Spokane newspaper, I looked up to see Jim and Saint Dorothy walking along the shore trail. He wore a proud ear to ear grin. She took mincing steps beside him, her arm protectively on his. He wore his white Stetson fishing hat, and she wore a "Please don't let him stumble look on her face."

"Morning pilgrim," I called, acknowledging his white John Wayne Stetson.

15

"Morning pilgrim," he beamed. "I'm ready to go fishing."

Saint Dorothy frowned disapprovingly but knew better than to question her forty year old man son. Thinking to ease her concerns I offered, "Why don't we try Huff Lake? It's only a hundred yards off the gravel top road. A cakewalk. Be a good first expedition."

"Tonight," he asked quickly, wanting to button it down before she could throw up any road blocks?

"Tonight's OK with me." Then looking questioningly at Dorothy and seeing no further objecting looks added, "I'll pick you up at seven. Give us an hour or better before dark, and we may be able to catch an evening hatch."

There was a three foot diameter log across the access trail at the lake, a shallow slough and tall grass to the shoreline. Things you normally think little of but serious obstacles for Jim. Using his rod case for a walking stick, Jim cursed and stumbled his way to the lake shore, each step bringing beads of sweat to his forehead. We set up where some fallen gray snags reached into the water. It is a small narrow lake. You can cast nearly across it. We lay our flies out along the weathered snags. You feel a little uneasy as the mossy ground undulates underfoot with the pressure of your casts. I was a bit concerned that Jim might lose his balance and tumble in. The waters which dropped off at his feet were eight or more feet deep. So I kept a watchful eye on him.

We caught and released a few small trout. We heard larger fish feeding, but they were not taking the mayflies that were dancing up and down over the water. We tried a series of dry flies but never did find what they were feeding on. My moose did not show, and we finally left.

Jim took the first trip well, but he was not ready for the rugged hikes into the alpine lakes when my grandboys, Mat and Nick, came out from the east for a visit. The Selkirk's once barren lakes had been stocked over the past twenty years with several species of trout.

The boys chose to try Hunt Lake first. because it held west slope cutthroat as well as the rare and exotic golden trout. Hunt Lake lies at a little over five thousand feet elevation. A two track, passable only by four wheel drive or pickup, takes you within a mile of the lake. From there it is a bitch of a climb up a forty five degree talus slope of granite boulders, some the size of a Mack Truck.

I thought of the sixty year old man who made the hike into the Selkirk peaks and dropped dead the next day. I wondered if I could handle the climb up the talus slope. But I wanted to walk in alpine meadows and see the cobalt waters of Hunt Lake again and have the grandboys experience it as I had as a boy. I told myself that I might not pass that way again.

The route up the talus slope was marked by red arrows and red circles surrounding a red dot splashed on the boulders. They reminded me of petroglyphs, and as petroglyphs they seemed in balance with nature. Ten thousand years from now archeologists will wonder what they meant.

My chest pained me at first, but then I climbed over the pain and was able to move upward at a steady pace. In places, we had to climb hand over hand, squeeze through narrow passages, and sometimes we had to jump from boulder to boulder. The air was thin, and I stopped now and then to catch my breath.

We finally broke out into a great granite walled cirque that had fingers of dwarfed whitebark pine reaching up the cracks and chimneys. We could see the lake nestled in the bottom of it.

At the edges of snow banks where the ground was moist, yellow alpine lilies and bear grass bloomed. Alpine fir grew up to the waters edge except for a rocky stretch along the southwest corner of the lake. At the far end of the lake was a small grassy meadow.

There was a chop on the water, the wind swirling in one direction and then another. A few fish were rising in one sheltered corner. There, a large boulder reached out from the trees allowing a short backcast. We pulled ourselves up on it. Not being able to see what the trout were taking, we each tried a different fly...Adams, Royal Wolf, Brown Hackle...hoping one would work. We took fish on all three. They were mostly small cutthroat but occasionally a fish of ten to twelve inches. The growing season is so short that the trout do not get much bigger. I had hoped to catch a golden trout, but we caught just the cutthroat.

We ate our lunch on the boulder, lay back in the warm sun, looked for mountain goats on the granite walls and crags. A small black bear came up behind us apparently drawn by the smell of our fish.

"Well, what do you think of all this," I asked the boys?

"Super papa," Matt replied. "I wish we didn't have to go back."

You do not want to leave. It is so deeply satisfying. You wish you could live there forever. But finally you have to leave before darkness catches you out on the talus slope.

The hike had gone well. No problems. So next we hiked into Standard Lake. This was a much longer hike, nine miles round trip, but on a well maintained Forest Service trail. The first part ran along Two Mouth Creek through a forest floor covered with dark green moss. There was a particularly picturesque stretch where the creek flowed over smoothly worn granite that ended in a falls of eight to ten feet.

Then the trail crossed over Two Mouth, and we had to hump across its rocky gorge on a smooth, weathered log. From there the trail switch-backed up the north face of Goblins Knob. It passed through patches of

17

huckleberries from which we snatched handfuls of berries as we strode along. Standard Lake lay just under the crest of the mountain. It was smaller than Hunt Lake, set in a rock bound depression. It did not have a visible outlet. The shore was more open with ample room for a back cast, easier to fish, but we had few strikes. The nearest we came to catching one of its cutthroats was a fish that tore free as I drew it up to the boulder on which I was perched. I would have liked to turn it free myself and felt a small disappointment.

We fished Petite Lake, just over the Washington border in the mountains just west of Priest Lake. There were two large beaver houses on it, and we did catch sight of beaver working around them. It was the first the grandboys had seen and a thrill for them. We caught and released a few cutthroat trout. A fisherman using a float tube joined us. I was surprised to see him moving backwards over the lake. But then I realized that he was using fins on his feet to propel himself, and it was a reasonable way for him to go. Three mule deer fed unconcernedly along the far shore.

We made the annual trek into grandpa's beaver dams on a stream whose name I will not mention. I still respect his penchant for secrecy. He and I first fished them sixty years ago. We took large cutthroat out of them then. I like to visit them and taste the nostalgia and feel the feelings when grandpa and I fished the waters together.

Some years if the beaver are not working the dam, the water is down and just a small stream remains in the meadow. This was the case. We took a few brookies by dapping our flies in the deeper water in the bends and under logs that stretched the stream.

Finally the grandboys' two weeks came to an end, and I drove them to the airport in Spokane. They were blue and I was blue. I watched their plane take off, and the easy tears of age came up.

One evening a few days later when Jim's side was stronger and the pain had subsided we took off for the fabled waters of Reynolds creek. The first problem we encountered was a washout in the two track and had to leave the car and walk. The second was a maize of logging roads that took off in all directions. We had to back track just once. The two track wound up through the hills passing one beaver meadow from which two mule deer bounded.

At last we reached the final turn to the right and the dip down into the creek bottom that the rancher had mentioned. Here the stream was little more than a trickle. It had been unusually dry for two years and the water table had fallen all over the Kaniksu. According to our calculations, the dam could be no more than a hundred yards upstream. There was a tangle of trees through which we plowed and broke out on a large beaver meadow. It appeared to be dry, but then we noticed a glint of water off to our left. We

18

made our way over through heavy grass and tangles of gray weathered logs that once floated in a great beaver pond.

The remnant pond was quite small, the water a walnut color. I saw one small fish rise for a may fly. I tried an Adams, then a gold ribbed Hare's Ear nymph which I promptly lost to a sunken log. The pond was deep. Perhaps seven feet deep and was interlaced with sunken logs.

Jim had been watching, and now he tied on his favorite fly, a black Wooly Bugger with a strand or two of silver ribbon among the black feathers. He quickly lost it to a log, then lost another and another. In the meantime, I lost a fly called the Undertaker, then tried a Blue Damsel because I had seen one dipping over the water.

Jim finally reeled in and said, "I'm getting out of here. I'm losing all of my best streamers. There's only one fish in here, if you actually saw one."

I was beginning to wonder if I had actually seen it, or if it had been a Damsel Fly or a play of light filtering through the trees. The light was beginning to fade as we crashed back through the trees to the two track.

I was enjoying the hike. I like to explore new country, and if in the process I take a trout or two so much the better. Whatever disappointment I had felt was gone, but Jim was quiet, grim.

I broke the silence, "That meadow had to be a huge pond once. Maybe even a small lake."

"Fabled waters. More like a desert," Jim said bitterly. "It was so dry there were oil wells and derricks all over the place and Arabs running around drilling for oil."

"Aw Jim, it's a great evening. We've seen some deer, some new country. Another year could be wet, the beaver back working the dam, the dam full and the fish down from the feeder creeks. I've seen it happen."

"That may be true," Jim replied. "But just once I'd like to catch some decent sized trout."

The next morning I was thinking about the last expedition into Petite Lake with the grand boys. Shortly after crossing the divide on our way out, a large black bear had bolted across the road ahead of us. We had stopped the car and got out to watch it scramble down the drop-off at the road's edge. I noticed a glint of water from what I suspected were beaver dams in the distance in the narrow valley below.

Later in the day, I drove up to the Priest Lake Ranger Station and picked up an aerial map of the region. It showed three ponds and a Forest Service two track that gave access to the area. The ranger said they held eastern brook trout. With a yellow marker, he indicated where the Forest Service had installed an iron gate across the road. Beyond was a bridge that crossed the stream that fed the beaver ponds.

19

He said, "You'll have to park your car here. Walk a short distance up the road and then cut cross country about a mile to the dams."
Simple. The only problem was the terrain never looks the way you visualize it from the map. And you inevitably get into alder swamps, and a Forest Service mile can be anywhere up to ten thousand feet.

I took my English Setter, Chain, for a walk the next morning and came upon Jim down on the beach reading his newspaper. I called out, "Morning pilgrim."

"Morning pilgrim. What's up?"

I told him what the ranger said, and he responded with firmness, "I'm tired of fishing barren beaver ponds."

By now we had lucked out on the fabled waters of Reynolds Creek, the fabled waters of Soldier Creek, the fabled waters of Horseshoe Bend on the Priest River that gave up two little whitefish and a seven inch rainbow trout.

"Count me out. No more beaver ponds."

"But Jim," I wheedled. "This is different. These dams are way up on the divide in virgin country that lies over the border in Washington. No one's coming way around from Washington to fish these beaver dams for a few little twelve or thirteen inch brookies. These are fabled waters, Jim."

"Where did you hear there were trout like that up there?"

"The ranger at the U.S. Forest Service said some fellow took several earlier this summer. What greater authority do you want?"

I could see he was weakening, and soon he capitulated. "It's against my better judgement, but OK I'll give it a try."

A short distance after we cut around the iron control bar the Ranger had mentioned, we came upon a game trail wandering off through an open Lodgepole Pine forest in the general direction of the dams. We took off on it and soon came upon some high piles of scat.

"Holy smoke, Jim. Look at the size of those piles."

"Big bear. Big pile."

"How do you know it's a bear?"

"I know those things."

"Touch it and see if it's warm. Find out if it's close by."

"No way. You touch it."

"No you're the authority. You know those things."

"I'll just whistle a tune. Let them know we're here. They'll get out of our way."

So we moved out along a ridge that paralleled the feeder creek, Jim whistling a monotonous tune. The first dam had little water in it. The second likewise. But the third was full to the brim with clear, sweet water. Large logs stretched out into the water, but there were several open casting lanes. A few fish were feeding. We caught fish of seven and eight inches, brookies, and Jim lost one he said was heavier. Then as the day heated up the pond went dead.

"You know, Jim," I mused when we got back to the car, "There have to be big trout in that pond. It's deep. Lots of insect life. The big ones must be holed up down at the bottom during the heat of day. We ought to slide in there the hour before dark when it's cool and those big brookies are feeding. The high terrain along that ridge top was open, and it only took us fifteen minutes to walk out. With flashlights, we would have no trouble getting out of there in the dark."

"I was thinking along those lines myself," Jim replied. "Let's give it a try."

The next day Jim stopped by early in the morning from picking up his newspaper at Hill's Resort. "Count me out on the Kalispel ponds. I was at Hill's bar last night having a couple Hales Ales with Hap. He's back from fighting fires down around Boise."

"Hap says that's grizzly country, and you're not going to get me to rub elbows with grizzlies in the dark. I think I'm going to have to find a new fishing partner who has a better handle on the fishing around here."

"Pilgrim," I countered, "Your problem is that you are a meat fisherman. You like dredging up those lake trout in Cavanaugh Bay. It's as exciting as pulling up a rubber boot filled with water. You don't appreciate the niceties of the sport. The rodwork. The beauty of the reflections of the mountains in the waters. The smell of a field of daisies or lupine. You do dress well, and that is important. Your Stetson is impressive. Your chocolate chamois shirt matched with your tan poplin trail pants is impeccable. But you must learn to smell the lupine, observe the flora and fauna, as it were."

"Bull shit as it were," he snorted. "Saint Dorothy says we have as much chance catching big fish as a fart has in a windstorm!"

"Jim! Your sweet mother couldn't have said that."

"Perhaps not," he laughed. "Perhaps with Hap back we can fish his top secret beaver pond. He took a three pound brookie out of it, and I caught two cuts twelve and fourteen inches early in June, before the accident."

"Oh ho! So you have been holding out on me!"

"No. You're the old timer who was fishing this country before Christ and supposed to know where all the big fish are. I didn't want to question your superior knowledge nor ruffle your delicate ego. Besides I wouldn't go unless Hap went with us or gave us permission."

"We'll have to fish in the evening," he continued. "So no one can see us because the pond lies in plain sight. Maybe tonight if Hap can get away."

We drove over in Hap's ancient pickup truck, front window a web of spidery cracks, body loose, upholstery comfortably worn, floor liberally sprinkled with beer cans and other debris. From the looks of the body, it had probably been the subject of the "beat me for a dollar event" at the logger's annual Kiwanis carnival in Priest River. In other words a man's car, a fish car, capable of taking you anywhere.

Hap pulled into a two track. We walked a couple of hundred yards to the pond. It looked more like a swamp than a trout pond. But up close I could see the water was clear. Fish were feeding and swallows and nighthawks were swooping over the open water. The pond was shaped like a tadpole, big belly ninety feet in diameter with tail that disappeared into a shallow brushy slough to the left. Across the pond a small stream emptied in and beyond the forest stretched forever.

It was cooling down and would be chilly. The tree tops caught the sun's last rays and were reflected in the pond. A pair of ducks of a nondescript color, maybe widgeons, moved unhurriedly out of the belly and up the tail. The dancing mayfly was dancing up and down over the water.

The trout would not take the matching dry fly. What they did like was the brown hackle, size twelve. The fly would be good for one or two fast bouts, and then you had to replace it with a fresh more appetizing one.

"Fabled waters, Pilgrim?"

"Um-hum," he answered, at the moment fully focused on a large brookie that was trying to force his way under an overhanging alder.
Just about the time it got too dark to see, Jim pointed across the pond and said quietly, "Look. There's your moose."

A cow moose and her two calves were standing on the far tree-line watching us. She stared impatiently, annoyed that we were in her private feeding grounds. She turned toward the calves, grunted, and they lay down in the fringe of grass, only their oversize noses showing. She waded in and began feeding. To hell with us.

We packed it in. We'd used most of our brown hackles anyway. We tucked our rods and fishing vests away. Hap popped three cans of beer. We leaned back against the friendly, comfortable old truck and sipped our beer.

Chapter 3

Along the Waterfront, Coolin, Priest Lake Idaho.

THE BEARDMORE STAGE ROBBERY

On September 9, 1914 at 3:30 PM, three masked bandits held up the Beardmore Stage Coach when it slowed down on the Finstad Grade three miles out of Priest River, Idaho.

Charles Wolcote Beardmore, owner of the stage coach came to Priest River from Oshkosh, Wisconsin at the age of seventeen by way of Grand Forks, Fargo, Bismarck, Livingston, Mammoth Hot Springs, Butte, Missoula, and Sandpoint. Much of the journey was made by bicycle with a few short hops by train. Being a practical man, he worked at various jobs along the way.

He had intended to settle in Butte but was involved in a fight at the B & B Smelter where he worked. It seems out of character for a man who later always appeared in a business suit and tie. It was probably a case of one of the toughs hazing the tenderfoot.

When he arrived in Priest River, early in the morning July 28, 1900, Priest River was experiencing rapid growth due to timber speculation in white pine timber lands north of town. Charles staked out a claim. Claims had to be filed in Coeur d' Alene, Idaho. He took the Great Northern to Spokane arriving late and missed his connection to Coeur d' Alene. He spent the night at the Pacific Hotel. There he saw a man he felt he had seen before, but he could not remember where.

The man was on the same train the next day, and as they neared the station he realized he had seen him looking over his claim. As the train slowed down at the depot, the stranger jumped from the train, and a race to the claims office was on. The stranger forged ahead, but as they started down a winding stairway to the claims office, Charles jumped over the banister, landed ahead, beating the stranger out and won the claim.

He immediately started logging off his land and floating logs down the Lower West Branch River to the mill in Priest River. He was later to buy the mill.

In 1902 he purchased the ST. Elmo Hotel. In 1903 he brought his bride, Lucy Gumaer, to the St. Elmo where they lived the remainder of their lives. In 1904 he purchased the Priest River Stage Line. The early stage was a four horse drawn wagon. It left from the St. Elmo and went twenty six miles up the old dirt and corduroy road to Coolin at the lower end of Priest Lake. The trip took all day stopping at the Prater's Halfway Station for a noonday farm dinner. There being no phones, Mrs. Prater never knew how many passengers would be on the stage. She always prepared enough food for however many passengers might come. Charles replaced the horse drawn stage coach in 1914 with a White Motor Coach cut in half and extended to seat eighteen passengers. It was involved in the holdup.

It was Leonard Luby from whom I first learned about the holdup. Leonard chuckled when he told me about it. Called it the late great stage coach holdup.

He said, "It was no smooth movie Wells Fargo Stage Coach holdup. More of a Laurel and Hardy comedy routine. My father, Mike, was on it. You remember him?"

"I sure do. I was always intimidated by him."

"You've got it. He intimidated everyone, even his family. He was a lawyer, Iron Mike. He probably intimidated the bandits."

"The holdup," he continued, "occurred about three miles out of Priest River when the stage slowed down coming up a steep grade in a densely wooded area. Three masked bandits jumped out of the undergrowth. Hugo Desmet, the driver, found himself looking down the barrels of two six guns and a rifle. The bandits ordered him to stop the stage. He did so promptly. They then ordered him and the seven passengers

24

to line up in the middle of the roadway. There were five men and two women. The man with the rifle stood guard and the other two proceeded to relieve them of their cash and jewelry."

Charles Beardmore and Stage

THOMAS F. LACY

"Mike said the bandits were obviously novices. They used white curtains for masks. One's red hair showed below his mask. The two who searched them were so nervous their guns shook. The only concern the passengers had was that they would accidentally discharge their guns. The passengers were able to drop much of their cash and jewelry into the dust on the road and cover it with their feet. The man who searched Mike got $12 in cash and overlooked a diamond pin valued at $150 and some more cash. The bandit's total take was $60 in cash and jewelry valued at $150."

"One of the bandits then fired his six gun four times into the engine of the stage. He ordered the passengers to walk up the road and not stop until they had covered a mile. The bandits then disappeared into the woods. After going a short way up the road, four of the men returned and worked on the engine, finally getting it started The passengers then returned about a mile toward Priest River when the motor stopped, and they had to walk the last two miles to report the crime."

A month later Mike Luby was called to the county jail to inspect two suspects. He said that their walk and height were the same as the masked bandits. He noted that one had red hair. They were being held on suspicion of robbing a driver of a car on a Bonner County highway of $100 and a watch. Mike said that he could not reach a definite conclusion as to their identity. They were not charged with the crime.

Because the stage was carrying mail, the crime was a federal offense, and postal authorities were called in to assist the sheriff. However, no one was apprehended until January 1, 1917 when Lonnie Eastley of Tweedie, Washington and Joe Bossio and Jean Naccarata of Priest River were arrested and confessed to holding up the stage. They implicated William Vane, one of Newport, Washington's wealthiest citizens. At one time he owned the town- site of Old Town and still owned much property there. He also owned an island ranch above Albeni Falls. Vane had previously lost a court case to Charles Beardmore and bore him a grudge.

Vane was arrested in Spokane at the offices of his lawyer with whom he was meeting regarding a perjury charge. Vane had testified to the innocence of a Carl Brink on a horse stealing charge. Vane called the charge a frame-up.

Eastley later confessed that he and Joe Bassio and Jean Naccarata met with Vane on his island. Vane claimed to be head of an organized gang of robbers. He tried to get Eastley to do other holdups. It was agreed that all four would split the take from the holdup.

They went back to Priest River to a cabin on the Priest Lake Road from which they operated. Vane furnished the guns, maps, lunch, and directions on how to commit the holdup. Eastley said the take was $28 or $29, five or six watches, and a mail sack they later burned.

Vane, Bossio, Naccarata, and Eastley were tried on June 14, 1917 in a federal court in Coeur d' Alene. Lonnie testified that Vane provided pepper and turpentine to cover their trail. He said that he did all the talking during the holdup for fear the two Italian's broken English would provide a clue to their identity. He testified that Vane was disappointed that the take was only $40 and not the $500 he expected. The case ended in a hung jury. A new trial was to be held in the fall term.

On November 28, Vane was convicted of conspiracy to rob United States mail and was sentenced to serve six years. Bossio and Naccarata were sentenced to serve four years each. And Eastley, who turned state's evidence, was sentenced to two years. May 23, 1918 Eastley's sentence was commuted by President Wilson. Wilson said, "Eastley was plied with liquor for two days and inveigled into the robbery by others."

Vane served six months of his federal sentence. He was released on a federal bond of $12,500 pending his appeal to the United States Supreme Court. Besides the federal charges, Vane was convicted on state charges of perjury and grand larceny in connection with the theft of a team of horses. The state convictions carried sentences of one to fifteen years.

Desperate at facing such long prison terms, Vane faked his death by drowning in the Pend Oreille River. The drowning was questioned and a federal marshal aided by local officers traced him to a cabin near Indian Creek on Priest Lake. He was asleep with a high powered rifle equipped with a silencer beside him. He was taken to the Pend Oreille county jail. On January 18, 1919 he committed suicide by taking strychnine.

Chapter 4

Chimney Rock from Granite Creek, Priest Lake, Idaho.

MUSHROOMING

Three climatic zones come together at Priest Lake; the Pacific Northwest, the Sub Artic, and the Rocky Mountain resulting in a vast garden of mushrooms, Matsutake, Shaggy Mane, Chanterelle, Boletus edulis, Meadow mushroom, Morel, Scarlet cup, Russula, Fly mushroom to name a few. There are hundreds of different kinds, some found only here.

In the fall of the year, the Spokane Mushroom Club sponsors a mushroom foray at Hill's Resort that draws mushroom enthusiasts from far and wide. One day is spent in the field studying and gathering different species. The mushrooms are displayed on long tables at the resort and are identified and labeled. It is an amazing sight, often more than 450 species have been collected.

Lois Hill is an avid and knowledgeable mushroom hunter. She knows the mushrooms, and she knows the country. She ran a two hundred mile trap line in the early days of Hill's Resort and appeared on TV's

"What's My line." I thought I knew the country, but she once showed me a mountain of crystals, another time where the wild hollyhocks grow, and still another time a uranium mine. The entrance to the mine had been filled with earth. Only a small opening remained at the top. I had to have a look and we clambered to the top. I crawled through the hole. Lois hung onto my feet to keep me from tumbling through. The tunnel turned almost immediately to the right and a bright light seemed to emanate from it. Radiation waves? It was eerie.

I backed out. "Lois," I said. "It's bright in there."

She crawled through the hole, and I hung onto her feet. She backed out quickly. "That's spooky." We hauled out of there. I've always wondered what was going on.

I believe the first time Lois took me hunting mushrooms was to a spot about an acre or two in size and a mushroom hunter's paradise. It was wooded and the earth black, rich. A faint trail led into it. Little light filtered through the canopy of trees. There was quite a bit of down timber, but here and there in the open areas we could see golden Chanterelles. There were four of us, Lois, Kahri Wigen, Mary Moss, and I. It was like an adult Easter egg hunt, the excitement, the joy bubbling over.

"Over here, look at these."

"Oh, my gosh! I can't believe it!"

"My oh my. Amazing!

Buckets were filling. Everyone was smiling. It was getting hot, but who cared. We could hardly take time out to go back and forth to the car and empty buckets. Finally we had the back end of the station wagon piled a mile high with those beautiful Chanterelle. Even the name is beautiful. Lois brought snacks and cokes. We had a tailgate party. Back at the resort we took pictures to record the event.

Later I returned the favor and took Lois fly fishing for cutthroat trout at one of my favorite fishing spots. We took the Four Wynns a good boat for fly fishing. It has an open fore and open aft providing two platforms to cast from. It was early evening, warm, the shadows reaching out from the shore, the water flat, and a few rings showing on the water. The trout were moving up and down the shore. I tied orange attractor flys to our leaders. We cast in front of the moving trout. She cast a rather nice fly. As I recall, the final score was two to one her favor.

Another time we picked on the other side of the road from the Chanterelles. Here the Boletus edulis grows, a very choice mushroom. Why they divide up the territory I don't know. The Boletus edulis side may be a little more open and perhaps somewhat dryer. It looks like a hamburger bun growing on a stalk out there. Some years are very good and some years you can't find one for love or money. But anyway it was a good year for the

Boletus edulis and we picked several buckets full. Some were up to nine inches in diameter.

The Matsutake mushroom is quite abundant around Priest Lake. It is an interesting mushroom. It is large, white and when you pull it up it has gray ash on the bottom of the stalk. It has a spicy taste and much desired for oriental cooking. It grows in mossy areas and you not only look for white mature mushrooms popping out of the moss but also rounded little mounds in the moss. Nine times out of ten if you part the moss you will find a white cap, a Matsutake about ready to pop.

One season the Matsutake crop was abundant. Lois got the bright idea of sending our surplus over to dealers in Seattle. The first shipment fetched twenty seven dollars a pound. As the season progressed, the price dropped to five dollars a pound. We made a few hundred dollars. We didn't get rich, but it was fun being paid for what we loved to do.

Alexander Smith, professor emeritus of botany at the University of Michigan and considered to be a leading authority in mushroom identification, spent several summers at the Priest Lake Experiment Station studying and identifying mushrooms in the area. He wrote the book, "The Mushroom Hunter's Field Guide." It is an excellent guide to the identification, edibility, time of fruiting, and where to look for many of the mushroom species. It is a good book to have with you when you are hunting mushrooms.

Alex told me that not everyone can eat a so-called edible mushroom. For example some people can eat brown cap morels and some people become ill from eating them. He advised, "When you are eating an edible mushroom for the first time, place a small piece on your tongue. If you feel no reaction, cook a cap and eat a quarter of it. If you have no reaction, eat more the next time, but never overindulge." He also told me not to mix species when collecting mushrooms.

Once Lois, Kahri, Mary, and I were picking Boletus edulis in an area of woods and cottages and doing quite well. The mushrooms lay among small trees which you had to squirm through, just off a road. I was beginning to wonder if mushrooms liked roads. We turned the corner of an abandoned cottage, and there in the yard was a gathering of strange mushrooms, orange balls on white stalks. Startling. On closer inspection you could see they were covered with white warts. Ugly. Ominous. Looks alone were enough to drive you off. Lois quietly said, "Don't get too close. They're the Fly Mushroom. Poisonous." I later referred to Alex's guide and it said, "A saucer of milk with a cap of A. muscaria (the Fly mushroom) soaked in it can be used to stun or kill flies." We retired to Mary Moss' for a bourbon. Her husband, Dick Moss, took a flash picture of our pile of Boletus edulis.

A mushroom expedition may unfold something like this:

Lois,   "Would you care to pick some white Chanterelles?"
Me,   "Love to."
Lois,   "John and Sharon can go."
Me,   "Great! When?"
Lois,   "High noon, tomorrow. Top secret place."
Me,   "Sounds good."
Lois,   "Blind folds, of course."
Me,   "You don't trust me!"
Lois,   "Why should I? I've only known you forty years."

(She doesn't mean it...mushroom hunting joke)

The top secret spot lay just off a well traveled black topped road. A two track ran through it. Lois pulled in far enough so that no one would notice us. It was open Lodgepole Pine, dry and flat. We pondered the heat and the dryness, and decided to give it a try as long as we had come this far. We spread out The delicious little devils were hunkered down in the Kinnikinnick, hard to see. We were finding them by onesies and twosies, and then John and Sharon came upon a nice little pocket. It was not a mother lode, and they soon cleaned it out. So we moved to the other side of the two track. We worked quite a piece of it, but didn't find a thing.

John suggested we try a spot where he once found a few white Chanterelles. It, too, was just off a well traveled black topped road. The road thing again. You may have noted that I have not given a precise description of the location of the spots where we have picked. Good spots are hard to find and can be picked over in a hurry. So it's become a rather clandestine operation, and you would no more divulge the location of a good spot than you would divulge the combination to your lock box. We scoured John's secret spot, but found only a few more. It, too, was dry.

I've never gone back. I still can see it all as clearly as though I were standing there. The times were good and I relive them often. Thanks for all of it.

Mary, Lois, Kahri

Jim, Dort, Loren, Author

Chapter 5

Camp Scene on Upper Priest Lake, Idaho.

HUCKLEBERRYING

I love to pick huckleberries. I don't know why. It's hot, sweaty, knee skinning, hard, dirty work. Maybe it's because it's so peaceful and quiet out there. And the pine needles smell so good. And a lovely deer may wander by or a fool hen may stop and stare at you. Then there are the huckleberry pies and the huckleberry pancakes.

Too, there is the camaraderie of the thing, Jim and Sandy and John and Sharon and Marion and Dot. Lois doesn't pick huckleberries much anymore. Says she picked too many in the early days of Hill's Resort. I did get a card from her one fall saying that she and Sandy and Bev got into some quarter size huckleberries on some mountaintop. Her huckleberry pie is to die for; open face, berries covered with a huckleberry glaze and topped with whip cream or ice cream.

The Kaniksu is one huge huckleberry patch. You can stop your car most anyplace and in a short time pick enough berries for a pie that night and pancakes in the morning. Then there are the special places, the places where you find nickel and dime size huckleberries. You keep your eyes open for them whenever you are driving the back-roads or walking the trails. You look for spots where moisture accumulates, small ravines, benches, depressions. And then there are those places that you stumble onto, a side hill facing south, the bushes short, scrubby, compact, loaded with those beautiful nickel and dime size berries. Some of the best spots are at high elevation and the best picking late in the season.

There are three different colors of huckleberries smoky blue, red and deep purple. The smoky blue are too bland, the red too tart, and the deep purple just right. The season usually starts in late June and goes into late September. The berries first ripen at around 2500 feet elevation. Then as the season progresses the berries ripen at higher and higher elevations until September when you will be picking at 5000 feet or better.

I hang my bucket on my belt and pick with both hands. The picking goes faster and my bucket fills faster. It also prevents tipping the bucket over. There is nothing more painful than tipping over a bucket of berries, and trying to pick the berries out of the needles on the ground.

I have been picking huckleberries since I was five or six years old. I was given a tin cup and told that if I picked enough berries we would have huckleberry pie or huckleberry grunt for dinner. That is what they called it…huckleberry grunt. Doesn't sound too appetizing does it? But it consists of sweet dumplings in a huckleberry sauce smothered in the thick cream of the day. Really quite good.

There was not a whole lot to do at Priest Lake in those days and huckleberrying was an important family activity. The forest was more open in Luby Bay then and the forest floor was carpeted with huckleberry bushes. So grandmother, mother, sister, and I would go out armed with tin cups, two gallon pail, and khaki hats draped with mosquito netting to pick huckleberries. Grandma was seventy-five years old, but spry, and could scramble over the down timber with the rest of us. We would hike up to the Indian Camping Grounds where the huckleberries were bigger and more abundant. We would return with a gallon of berries for huckleberry pie, pancakes, jam and…huckleberry grunt. As time passed and roads were built into the backcountry we moved on to richer patches.

In all the years I have picked huckleberries, I have never looked over a bush and found a bear picking huckleberries with me. The huckleberry is highly nutritious and an important part of a bear's diet. They fatten up on them for the long period of hibernation. I have heard of people who have come upon a black bear in a huckleberry patch. The bear always turned tail and ran. There are still grizzly bears in the Kaniksu, and I would just as soon not run into one in a berry patch.

Good huckleberry patches are closely kept secrets and lead to rather peculiar behavior. There is this one mountain where quite a few of the folks pick. A two track goes all the way to the top. It is perhaps fifteen miles long. On the way up you pass parked cars and the folks busily look the other way hoping you won't notice them. You do not stop for a friendly chat. You charge straight by. Where they are picking, the berries are small anyway. You hope they will not follow you.

The higher you go the worse the road gets. At last you are hanging on the side of the mountain and you are rolling back and forth over boulders protruding out of the road that threaten to throw you overboard or tear out your oil pan. Jim and Sandy ride lookout for prime patches. No one would go up there but a huckleberry picker. But the berries are of the nickel and dime size. When you get to your secret place and a car is parked across the way you don't go over there and glad hand them, ask who they are and where they are from and so forth. You slide into the little opening where you have parked for years, grab your buckets, hats and mosquito dope and melt into the undergrowth. You don't want them to know exactly where you will pick, and I am sure they don't want you to know exactly where they will pick. You want to feel you are alone out there in the wide -open spaces and they feel likewise.

I like to find a nice warm spot and a nice patch of nickel and dime size berries and sit down and pick. Sitting down you can look up and see any berries that are hiding from you under the leaves. The only drawback is that you may sit on berries and get purple bottom. But I don't object to a little stain on my Levis. They are old anyway. First I eat a few of the big juicy berries. When I hear the berries plunking into the other buckets, I start picking. We do not talk a lot, and if we do it is in a low voice. It does not seem right to break the stillness. That is to enjoy. You may hear a rock cony chirp, but that is all right. If someone is quiet too long, you know that he or she is into a patch of the nickel size berries and you slide over to see if you can help out. They may tell you to find your own huckleberries. But if you will hang in there they will soon be talking animatedly about the size and the deep purple color and how tasty they are.

You pick a bucket of berries enough for a pie or two, huckleberry pancakes, and perhaps some huckleberry jam. Huckleberry jam on toast in the wintertime is priceless. You take pictures of everyone holding his or her bucket of berries, grinning ear to ear. Everyone is always grinning ear to ear in those pictures. You leave quietly.

You see more and more people up there every year. Things are changing. Some day, someone will come up there with a hot dog and pop wagon, sell tickets, souvenirs, maps, and give lectures on how to pick huckleberries. But thank God we saw it at its best.

Chapter 6

Lion Head Bay and Lookout Mountain, Priest Lake, Idaho.

BEAUTIFUL PRIEST LAKE

Excerpt From Bert Lacy's Memoirs

Our first trip to Priest Lake was in 1917. At the time, Priest Lake was 85 miles from Spokane via dirt roads. People figured five to six hours by car and two days by horse drawn rig to Priest Lake. A co-worker on the Spokesman Review, Earl Smith, and I decided to make the trip one weekend taking our families. As the round trip seemed too far for one day, we decided to leave Saturday afternoon and drive forty miles to Diamond Lake, camp there overnight, and drive on to Priest Lake the next day.

It was a hot summer day. I had a new Elgin car, and when I got half way to Diamond Lake the water was boiling. I was delayed a half hour getting water and cooling down the engine. At Diamond Lake, we cooked our dinner over an open fire. We slept on folding army cots.

The next morning we had a big breakfast of bacon and eggs and cinnamon rolls. Instead of backing my car out of the campground, I drove onto the sandy beach and soon was stuck. It took Earl and me over a half hour to get the car out. At the main highway, we found a road gang had just put four inches of sand and gravel on the road. We had to run in low gear all the way to Newport.

At Newport we ferried across the Pend Oreille River which was wide at this point. We soon had to traverse a rocky outcrop overlooking the Albeni Falls. Here the road was cut into the rocky hillside. To our right it dropped down several hundred feet to the falls. It was a spectacular view, but it put butterflies in our stomachs. The road was a single lane and no turn outs. I wondered what I would do if I met a car coming down. I certainly could not back down, and the other driver could not back up. Fortunately we met no one and were soon safely in the little logging town of Priest River.

Earl stopped to have his car checked. I told him I would drive slowly on. In about a half hour, I came upon the Priest River which originates at Priest Lake and empties into the Pend Oreille River a short way above the town of Priest River. Here there were two roads heading north. One ran along the river, and one up a hill. I took the hill road. I waited nearly an hour at a scenic overlook for the Smiths to catch up. Finally I drove back to the service station. I was told the Smiths had left an hour ago and evidently had taken the river road. I then took the river road to Coolin, a small village at the south end of Priest Lake.

We found the Smith's down on the beach admiring the fabulous view of Priest Lake. A man stopped by. Said he was Leonard Paul. He was very friendly, pointed things out to us. Said the little island we could see to the right was Four Mile Island. That it was just four miles north of Coolin. Beyond was Baritoe, and the hazy blue mountains far to the north lay in Canada. We asked about the quaint two story house with the stone drinking fountain out front. He said that it was Mrs. Handy's hotel, the Idaho Inn, and that we should taste the water in the well, the purest and sweetest in all the world. A small log building had caught our eye. He said it was his general store. He invited us to stop in if we had time and he'd show us around.

We had a picnic lunch on the beach, and then wandered over to Leonard Paul's store. The logs were weathered a dark brown and the chinking and trim were white, very attractive. Inside there were deer and mountain goat mounts on the walls and a large bear skin on the floor. There was everything from calico to shoes, overalls, long underwear, tea, flour, eggs, kerosene lamps, kerosene oil, candy, hardware, snowshoes, Indian moccasins, everything a homesteader, a miner, a trapper might need. He put up grubstakes for the miners, supplies for the Forest Service, and supplies for the logging camps. It was a frontier store for a frontier region.

We inspected the W.W. Slee steam boat that had just come in at the dock, and we drank from Mrs. Handy's spring, the sweetest water in all the world, It was three o'clock and time to return to Diamond Lake. There was a stretch of road a short way out of Coolin called the Jack Pine Flats. The trees were tall, straight, and came right up to the road. The road was straight as a die for over a mile. It was like looking down a great hall.

Jack Pine Flat Road to Coolin, Priest Lake, Idaho.

THOMAS F. LACY

The next morning we had breakfast, folded up camp and set out for Spokane. I followed Earl. Halfway to Spokane I ran over a large spike, six inches long, that flattened one of my new tires. Earl did not see me stop and drove on. He finally noticed I was not behind, and returned to see what was wrong. I was struggling to change the tire. In those days, we could count on having a flat or two on any long trip. We changed the tire and drove into Spokane.

Our son, Tom, was born in 1918 and we did not get back to Priest until the summer of 1921. Mike Luby, a Spokane attorney, who built the first cabin in Luby Bay in 1911 offered it to us for two weeks. We were delighted and accepted his invitation.

We arrived in Coolin early one afternoon. We intended to rent a boat and motor, but they were all taken. However, the W.W, Slee Steamboat was going up the lake shortly, and they would take us. They loaded our two weeks supplies, and hooked on a twelve foot rowboat and we started up the lake. About a mile out, the steamer blew a piston, and we could not move.

The crew loaded our supplies in the rowboat, and we started out to row to Luby Bay. There were six of us; Mary, Tom and Jeanette and Grandma and Aunt Grace. It was a six mile haul. When we rounded the point at the Woodrat Mine, our distant relative Grace Weller who owned one of the cottages in the bay spied us. She came out in their boat and motor and pulled us in.

Mike's cabin was twelve feet square. There was in addition a twelve by twelve foot tent with wood floor and three foot wood walls. The cabin was the kitchen. It had a wood burning cast iron cook stove that took off the early morning and evening chill. And there was a hand made wooden picnic table with a bench on either side.

The first night Mary and I were asleep in one of the tent beds. Around twelve o'clock we were awakened by something hitting against the wooden tent frame. The next morning we learned from the Wellers that it was a woodrat, an animal with a large rope-like tail, striking the tent frame. The Wellers told us not to leave jewelry lying around as they would take it to their nest.

We got up with the sun shinning bright in a blue sky, a forty foot wide white sandy beach in front of us, a deep blue lake six miles wide and the Selkirk Mountain range rising seven thousand feet high across the lake. There were five islands dotting the water. We soon forgot our troubles of the previous day.

I became so sold on building a cabin that I worked three days clearing the lot next to the Wellers. I accumulated three large piles of brush on the beach, each over ten feet tall. I planned on building the next spring.

After I returned home and considered the long drive and the poor roads, I decided against it.

However, we did vacation the next summer at Priest Lake. We rented a big one room, barney cabin from Fred Snider in Kalispel Bay, one mile north of Luby Bay. The cabin had three holes in the roof. When it rained we used a tub, a dishpan, and a bucket to catch the water. But what could you expect for $7 a week.

Grace Weller came to visit us Friday of the first week of our stay to tell us she was going home Sunday and wanted us to use their cottage for our second week. We were delighted and moved over. Their cabin had one room ten by sixteen feet with a screened in front porch eight by sixteen feet. There was a wall bed, cast iron wood burning stove, and kitchen counter in the one room and a wall bed on the porch. There was also a large sleeping tent with wood floor and three foot wood walls.

Charlie Robinson, a banker in Spokane, also had a cabin in Luby Bay. There were just four cabins in the bay at that time including the McWilliam's cabin. Charlie convinced me I should build next to him. I worked three days clearing the lot next to him and again accumulated three huge brush piles. They made grand bonfires in the evening. We toasted marshmallows and watched the orange harvest moon come up over the Selkirks. My it looked large.

I fully expected to build on this lot the next spring of 1923. Around Christmas time, I received a call at my office from Ernest Weller advising me that they were moving to Denver early in 1923 to go into business with his father-in-law, and he offered his cottage to me for $250. I told him I would talk it over with the folks that night. The next morning before nine I was at his office with the check for $250.

A blacksmith in Rosalia, Washington made a sixteen foot cedar planking four hundred pound boat to sell for only $125. They delivered one to me at Priest Lake for the 1923 season. I bought a new five horsepower Elto motor for it and used the boat for twenty five years. We called it the Mary for my wife. I replaced it in 1948 with a sixteen foot solid mahogany 95 horsepower two seated Chris Craft.

Priest Lake is twenty one miles long. The thoroughfare connecting it with the upper lake is two miles long, and the upper lake is three and a half miles long. The thoroughfare was shallow in parts at this time, and we would have to get out and push the boat. On both sides were tall pines and cedar and ferns and fireweed and some yellow flower. We think the twenty seven mile boat ride is number one in the Pacific Northwest.

In the early twenties, we would see deer come down to both ends of the bay to drink. We once saw a black bear swim across the bay from one point to the other. Priest Lake was a wonderful place for the children. Our daughter Jeanette and our son Tom loved Priest Lake, and were eager to get back each summer for two months. They were swimming in the lake most of the day, coming out for lunch or to warm up around the cast iron stove. Priest Lake is a cold lake. There were the Robinson, the Luby, the McWilliams, the Weller, the Davis children, all one big family. They always had some project going from hiking, rowing, swimming, berry picking, cards, looking for arrowheads, to making clay objects from a local gray clay.

Tom and I trolled for cutthroat and dolly varden trout in the bay. The trout were abundant in those days, and it was easy to catch two or three one and a half to two pound fish for dinner. When Tom was about ten years old, he developed a desire to fish the streams. Every other day he and I would drive up to one of the streams on the west side of Priest Lake. We first discovered West Branch and fished around the old Low homestead. We also hiked into the beaver dams on upper West Branch. In those days the road ended just beyond Low's, and a hike into upper West Branch was into primitive country. The fishing was exceptional. We could take a limit of trout from one beaver impoundment.

We also fished Granite Creek, often driving up in the late afternoon for the fly fishing. We would usually catch cutthroat trout eight to ten inches and occasionally tie into a lunker cutthroat or dolly varden. Kalispel Creek was good for eastern brook trout and an occasional big cutthroat. But of all the streams, Lamb Creek was our favorite. We had some great fishing for eastern brook trout in the early days before they blew out the big meadow dams. We fished the Last Hope Ranch, Elmer Henchel's ranch and the old Graham ranch, and took big, beautiful, dark beaver pond brookies.

We took two to three day camping trips to the Upper Lake. We would take a mattress from the cottage and sleep under the stars. The cutthroat fishing was excellent. We could take two or three pound trout to cook on spits over an open fire at night. Few people got up there then, and it was still primitive. We had deer come to water near our campsite. We would hear the mournful call of the loons. We heard a loud mysterious sound coming from the next bay. We investigated it but found nothing to account for it. We learned later from Jim Low that it was the warning sound a beaver makes by slapping its tail on the water.

Huckelberrying was a favorite family undertaking. We would drive up into upper Lamb Creek taking a picnic lunch with us. A few hours picking would net several gallons. Tom and I would scout out the good patches, then take Mary, Jeanette and Aunt Grace to them. Usually once a summer Mary and I would take a two day trip to the Upper Lake and camp out. We would hike a few miles up Plowboy Mountain to some exceptionally fine huckleberry patches. We could fill a gallon pail in no time.

THOMAS F. LACY

The family enjoyed hiking. Jeanette and her friends hiked up Indian Creek to Chimney Rock, to the lookout on Binarch Peak, and to the two lookouts at the south end of the bay. Tom hiked all over the Selkirk Range. His first hike to Hunt Peak he made alone leaving our cabin about five in the morning and returning at seven in the evening. He told his mother and grandmother that he was going with Colonel Tucker's son. Colonel Tucker headed the CCC camp in Kalispel Bay. There was no Colonel Tucker's son. Grandma was so impressed she got them Hershey bars. For some reason Mary got up to see him off in the Mary, and watched until he got up to the Indian Campground. Instead of going after Colonel Tucker's son he turned and went across the lake alone. In those days there were grizzly bear in that country and there were sheer drops of a thousand feet on the east slope of the Selkirks. Mary had to sweat it out all day, until he got home safely that night.

Jim Low homesteaded eighty acres behind us. This was in 1923. He cleared about a half acre of land and built a log cabin and log barn on it. Tom and his friend Ed McWilliams liked to visit Jim and get a sample of his mulligan stew. Late in August Jim came by our cabin one Sunday morning and after considerable hemming and hawing let me in on a big secret. He had shot a deer during the night. He asked if I would like a roast. I quickly agreed and accompanied him up to his small log barn where he had the deer hung. We cut off a roast and Mary cooked it for Sunday dinner. That was our first venison, and as I recall it was quite strong.

In those days, there were great runs of white fish up most of the streams emptying into Priest Lake. The runs occurred in October. We came out to the cabin one October for the week-end, and as I walked around the rear of the cabin, I saw four large apple boxes filled with freshly caught white fish. I told the folks we would have white fish for dinner as I suspected they belonged to Jim Low. So I picked out five fish. When Jim came by the next day, I told him I took five of his white fish. He insisted that I take a dozen to town.

The next fall Jim Low took his wife Myrtle, Mary and me across the lake to Hunt Creek one evening to fish for white fish. We took a coffee pot and kept it hot over a campfire, for it is cold that time of year. The pools were filled with fish. But they were elusive and it took a little practice before I could catch them. You use long handled dip nets and carry a lantern to see them. I filled an apple box with the whitefish.

Jim Low took me to lunch once at one of the Diamond Match logging camps where one of his brothers worked. We took the old narrow gage railroad up Kalispel Creek to camp #2 on Bath Creek. The tables were heaped with food. There were several kinds of meat, many dishes of vegetables, rolls, pastry, cakes, fruit, and coffee. The men ate almost exclusively with their knives, even heaping peas on them. It was from Jim's brother that we learned about the hidden beaver dams on Lamb Creek. We fished them in the late twenties, and were probably the earliest fishermen on these ponds. They were filled with cutthroat trout.

On the opening day of fishing, usually around April 20th, I used to take Les Bain and "Sad Slim" Smith up to the lake for a weekend of fishing. We trolled in the bay and would usually catch fifty to sixty fine cutthroat trout. We did this for a number of years.

Two small resorts were started in Luby Bay in the summer of 1924, Jim Low's Resort and Hampton's Luby Bay Resort. Jim built a small log cabin for himself and four small log cabins for rental. They were sparsely furnished with furniture he built. The Hamptons came from WallaWalla. There was not a passable road built into Luby Bay at that time and the Hamptons had to haul their lumber in two miles on a horse drawn log sled from a mill on the county road.

In 1928, Jim Low attended a Forest Service auction sale near the mouth of Granite Creek. They were offering 1800 feet of shore starting 600 feet south of the mouth of Granite Creek. Jim made the first and only bid of $450. The Forest Service talked for nearly an hour, and decided to sell it to Jim for $450 with $45 down and ten years to pay the balance. Jim moved his operation in Luby Bay up to his newly acquired land. He built a log lodge and fourteen log cabins on the north half of his land and operated it as Low's Resort. He also excavated a slough and built covered storage with exit to the lake.

Earl Farris bought Jim's Luby Bay resort from him in 1928. He ran it until 1946 at which time he sold it to George Hill.

Hampton only ran the Luby Bay Resort for a couple of years I believe. He developed back trouble and sold out to Will Schneider. Will added a small grocery store and in turn sold out to George Richter and his brother Carter Carlson. They ran it for several years, and added several cottages and a large lodge. The Richters sold the resort to a Mrs. Tim. Her son, Bob, ran the resort for several years, adding four cabins. George Hill bought the resort in 1960, adding it to the already large Hill's Resort. A few years later George moved the Luby Bay Resort lodge building down and joined it to his lodge building. He added a beautiful dining room and kitchen between the two lodge buildings. This made Hill's Resort the largest and finest in the Kaniksu.

From 1900 on there has been much logging. Large sections of the country west of Priest were logged off. The logs were dumped into the water at the south end of the bay. These were gathered in large log booms and towed to the outlet of the Priest River by steamboat. With a full boom the boats hardly seemed to move and took many hours to move the logs

down to the outlet. J.B. Slee brought the first steamer to Priest Lake, the
Kaniksu. Around the turn of the century he built a larger steamer the W.W.
Slee. E.J. Elliott built the steamer Tyee on the beach at Coolin in 1926
which made tourist runs in season and hauled log booms.

Archibald and Hansen both homesteaded land adjacent to the
intersection of the Luby Bay and West Branch roads. Dinty Murphy's
homestead was in the southeast corner of the intersection. Archibald built a
small building at the intersection, about sixteen by twenty four feet, and
operated a grocery in it for several years. Later Vander Vert purchased the
corner and enlarged the building and added a bar and dance floor. He
renamed it Van's Corner.

Around 1930, Bud Thompson built the Cedars just south of Van's
Corner. It had a large bar and catered to lumberjacks. He sold the Cedars to
Mille and her husband. Mille tended bar, told stories, and could swear like
the boys. I went in one day to locate my woodman. She did a lot of
swearing and thought I was a preacher.

Elmer Henchel was another old Timer. He came to Priest Lake
from St. Joe, Missouri around 1910. He homesteaded land about a half mile
up the Lamb Creek road. He raised strawberries and vegetables, and sold
them to summer residents in Luby Bay. The children followed him about
because they loved to hear him say, Ya Ya Oh Ya. They named him Ya Ya,
the Strawberry King.

Fred Snyder came around the turn of the century and homesteaded
over a half mile of choice shoreline in Kalispel Bay. He built a number of
rental cottages and had a small grocery for his renters and summer people.
A man called Helm homesteaded a half mile of shoreline east of Fred
Snyder. Bud Thompson bought Helm's lake shore property in 1930, and
built a large lodge and dining room on a picturesque sandy point there.
Byron Stephen, a boat builder from Spokane, built the Priest Lake Marina at
the south end of Kalispel Bay around 1940. It consisted of covered docks for
summer boat storage, winter storage for 60 boats, a machine shop, and a fine
second floor apartment with a picturesque view of the bay and the Selkirk
Mountains.

In the early thirties, the CCC's came to Kalispel Bay. There were
over one hundred boys from large eastern cities, New York, Philadelphia,
Boston, and others. They built the large log cabin for the U.S. Ranger
Station in Luby Bay. Jim Low called it the million dollar ranger station,
because it took so long to build.

Tom became acquainted with some of the boys. They were fine
young men. One of the boys taught Tom how to make twig furniture from
white birch and red willow. He made and sold several settees. He made one

for his mother which has always had a prominent place in front of our stone fireplace.

In the evenings, many of the boys from the CCC camp would stroll down the path in front of our cabin. When one of them was asked how he liked the lake, he replied, "It's God's country, because he's the only one who would want it."

Chapter 7

Thoroughfare, Priest Lake, Idaho.

OLD MAN WILLIAMSON

Old Man Williamson was the Forest Guard at Luby Bay in the early '20s, a white-haired, crusty old bastard. He was the kind of man who owned an Airedale, a bear hunting fighting bully.

Every morning about 9 o'clock Old Man Williamson and Scar would walk past our cabin on fire patrol. Scar pranced ahead like a prize fighter doing his roadwork, challenging any and all dogs to go a few rounds with him.

On Tuesdays Old Man Williamson made a twenty-mile fire patrol through the southern part of his district, and on Thursdays he made a twenty-mile fire patrol through the northern part. On the other days of the week, he would walk up Lookout Trail each morning to two rocky promontories on a ridge at the south end of the bay and, if it were hot and dry, again in the afternoon.

The two promontories were called Lookout One and Lookout Two. It was a two mile round trip, not too difficult for children. Occasionally he would allow sister Jeanette and me and the Robinson and McWilliams children to tag along. He would admonish, "No running nor horseplay on the trail. Walk quietly and slowly, and perhaps we'll see a fool hen or a deer." He was a man who inspired respect, and we would be quiet in hopes of seeing wild animals.

From the lookouts, we looked down on the people walking and swimming and the boats drawn up on the beach. We would marvel that they looked so small from that height. We could look into Kalispel Bay to the north of Luby Bay and down on Kalispel and Little Papoose and Baritoe Island. It was a whole new perspective and feeling for us, like the first time we skipped or jumped or turned a somersault.

But these were the few times that the sunshine of his soul shone through the dark clouds that he wore. I do not recall him smiling or joking or stopping to chat with my parents nor waving as he walked past each morning. He was a loner and satisfied to live within himself.

His job was finding forest fires. If they were small, he put them out himself. If they were large, he reported them to the ranger district headquarters in Coolin on his crank telephone. Jim Ward, the district ranger, would then send fire fighters to put the fire out. If the fires were in the backcountry, they could become quite large before the fire fighters could get to them. Occasionally a fire would burn out of control until the fall rains put it out.

The guard station where old Man Williamson lived was once a houseboat, now drawn up on dry land. It rested on large logs. There was a tiny porch at the front. Off the porch was a pole from which the American flag flew. The building was painted a dark brown with white trim and looked official.

When Old Man Williamson and Scar were off on patrol, we could peek inside but never had the courage to go in. It was dark and forbidding like the man himself. There was a large, cast-iron cook stove along one wall with bake oven and warming oven above in the single room. A sourdough can rested on the back of the stove. Beside the stove was a bucket of water with a long handled dipper sticking out. Often he could be seen to walk out on his dock, dip a bucket of water and return to his house. The water in Priest Lake was so pure and clear you could drink it.

There was a small dining room table and two chairs, rough hewn benches and stools in the room. In one corner was an iron cot and in another corner was a rough hewn desk where I imagine he made out and kept his reports. There were a few kerosene lamps with glass bowls and glass chimneys. The floor was worn but scrubbed clean. The whole was neat…neat as the man was about himself.

At the time, I had a Boston bulldog, a little mind-your-own-business kind of dog. Buddy was a warm, friendly little fellow and my best friend and constant companion. Every time he and Scar would meet on the trail that ran along the lakeshore, Scar would growl and challenge Buddy to a fight. But gentleman that he was, Buddy would ignore the bully's cheap shots.

One day Scar, after sniffing Buddy fore and aft, jumped him and forced Buddy to the ground. Buddy sank his teeth in Scar's throat, but Scar being larger and stronger shook him off, and they tumbled end over end to the water's edge.

Father hearing the fighting, rushed out of the cabin and shouted, "Damn it, Williamson, call off your dog. Buddy's no fighting dog."

But Williamson shot back, "Let 'em fight it out. It's been a long time coming."

Father picked up a piece of driftwood and tried to force the two dogs apart. But he couldn't separate them, and he couldn't pull the two dogs apart without getting bitten. Scar forced the fight into the water and held Buddy under water until he went limp. Father waded in and pulled Buddy out, carried him in his arms up to the cabin and wrapped him in a blanket. Buddy was still breathing, but he couldn't eat when Mother offered him warm milk with toast in it.

The next morning when I called for Buddy, Father took me out to a small copse of trees behind the cabin and showed me Buddy's grave. "Tommy," he said, "Buddy died during the night."

"Why did he have to die?" I sobbed.

"He fought bravely, but his heart must have given out, Tommy."

He didn't mention that it had all been senseless and cruel and Scar was a vicious brute and Williamson not much better, for I was too young to understand.

That Buddy was brave, I could understand. I never wanted to forget him, so we built a cross from two boards and carved his initials on it and pushed it into the soft earth. We picked some Indian paint brush flowers, blue lupine and white daisies, put them in a can filled with water from our old, red hand pump and placed it on his grave.

Old Man Williamson continued to walk past our cabin every morning on patrol. He did not apologize nor say he was sorry for Buddy's death. He held the fire guard job for a few more years and then retired to his homestead at the outlet of the Priest River to the west of Coolin. He built a few cabins to rent and lived comfortably on the rental income and the produce from a small garden and orchard.

We heard little of him until the summer of 1926. That was a dry year in the Kaniksu, and lightning from an August storm that moved in from the west started several fires. One fire north of Priest River took out a lookout tower and threatened the town itself.

Old Man Williamson

Another fire that had started in the mountains to the west of us was threatening Kalispel Bay. Smoke from the fire was so thick we couldn't see across Priest Lake. Papoose and the other islands were blotted from view. The smell of smoke was heavy in the air.

A strong wind came up and the fire burned out of control. In the evening, Jim Ward came down the bay and warned all of the summer people that the Kalispel Bay fire would take out that bay and was headed for Luby Bay.

"We've built a trench from the lake north of you over the hills to the West Branch Road and have started a backfire. We hope it will burn everything between the trench and the main fire and pinch it off."

"But there is no certainty we can stop it. So take what you can in your boats and bury the rest in the sand. Then go down to Fred Williamson's. You'll be safe there."

Williamson. I still hated the man for what he had done. I could still hear him say, "Let them fight it out." And I could still see Scar holding Buddy under the water. I detested the thought of staying with him. I looked to Mother for some answer, but she was already taking precious personal items out of bureau drawers, and seeing me standing there said impatiently, "Get busy. Bring boxes and suitcases out of the shed to put things in. Pick out things you want to keep."

"You've forgotten Buddy," I cried, tears welling up.

And then she came and put her arm around me and said, "No, Tommy, I haven't forgotten."

"I hate the man," I said. "I don't want to stay with him."

"Tommy, we mustn't carry hate in our hearts or we become like Mr. Williamson," she said softly. "We must try to understand. Perhaps there was a great sadness or hurt in his life that causes the anger he carries. We all loved Buddy. But we cannot let our love for Buddy and his death become a cancer in our souls that spreads."

Then she brushed the hair back on my forehead and the tears away that had gathered on my cheeks, kissed me and said, "We must try to understand the Williamsons and forgive and forget. And now we must get back to packing. It will soon be dark."

We put our most prized possessions in the Mary, named after mother. Mattresses, cooking utensils, canned food, furniture we placed in several piles on the beach, laid blankets over them and covered the piles with sand.

The sun was setting as we cranked up the Elto outboard motor on the Mary and headed out into the bay. We turned for one last look at our beloved cabin, and there standing among the mounds were Mike Luby and

Charley Robinson, their heads bowed, their hats held over their hearts. It had the appearance of a graveyard.

When we drew even with the point at the Woodrat Mine, we could see into Kalispel Bay. It was all ablaze, fire boiling up and black smoke reaching into the sky. The fire had reached a height of land above the beaches, and as we watched, marched down the slope to the cabins along the shore. The heat was so great that cabins exploded into flames, and for a few brief moments the windows stood out black and then the cabins disappeared.

The fire had crowned and was moving at high speed among the tree tops. The only things that could stop it were the waters of Priest Lake and Jim Ward's backfire.

We sat watching, mesmerized by the fire's awesome power...the towering swirling flames, the shower of orange sparks that reached far out into the bay, the reflections of the fire on the waters surrounding us. A flotilla of boats had gathered, refugees from both Kalispel and Luby Bay, watching the fire. Then Mother said, "We must leave before it becomes too dark to get through the shoals in front of Mr. Williamson's."

The water there was not over two feet deep and mined with large boulders that could tear out the bottom of a boat. As we approached the shallows, Mother cut the speed of the motor to where we were scarcely moving and said, "Tommy, your eyes are sharp. Crawl up on the prow and guide me through the boulders." I felt so proud of the trust placed in me that I temporarily forgot about Old Man Williamson.

In the gathering darkness, the boulders were vague dark shapes against the lighter sandy bottom of the lake, and here and there larger boulders broke the surface. I would shout, "left" and point to a submerged boulder or, "hard right." The Mary was heavily loaded, rode low and sluggish in the water, once we bounced broadside off a rock, but her sides were strong, built of narrow strips of inch thick cedar and no damage was done.

As we drew near the outlet, the water deepened, and we could feel a current building up as the water rushed to leave the lake and enter the riverbed. There was a rapids but a short distance downriver. To the left was Old Man Williamson's dock. The trick was to cut across the current and at the same time avoid being sucked into the rapids below. Mother gunned the motor, made a sharp left across the current and swooped into a landing alongside the dock.

We had been so engrossed that we hadn't noticed Old Man Williamson standing on the dock watching us. He tied the Mary up and then said. "Well done, Mrs. Lacy. Welcome to Pawnee Ranch."

There was a touch of warmth in his voice, and he even smiled, something we had never seen before. Mother smiled up at him and said, "Well, thank you Mr. Williamson. Did Jim Ward reach you?"

"Yes, he said you were coming. The cabins are taken, but I can put you up in my ranch house. There is a bedroom for you ladies, and I can put a cot in the living room for Tommy."

I didn't like him calling me Tommy, nor implying that we were old friends. I didn't like staying in his house, but Mother said, "That is very kind of you. Thank you."

He reached down, helped Grandma then Mother then Jeanette onto the dock. I jumped out before he could help me. His house was set back from the beach on a bench that had a long view up the lake past Baritoe and Four Mile Islands all the way to Lookout Mountain. There was an open porch across the front and immediately within a large room that combined a living area in the foreground with kitchen and dining to the rear. The ceiling was low, and I remember the room being warm and comfortable. There was a fireplace and on the walls deer racks and grouse fans. Before the fireplace was a black bear rug and some of the furniture was upholstered with cowhide from which the hair had not been removed. The cowhides were tan and white and black and white. There were even white curtains at the windows.

Beyond was an open hall with bedrooms on either side. One of these he showed to Mother, and I heard her exclaim, "White sheets and such quaint down comforters. You didn't make these yourself, did you?"

"No, they were handed down."

He told us to make ourselves comfortable, and he would remove the things from our boat and put them in our room. After he left, Grandma said, "He is so different. Kindly. I felt he was pleased to see us and have us here."

"Yes, I noticed it too. He's a different man than he was two years ago. Whatever it was, I'm happy it's over for him," Mother said. After retrieving our things, he set up an army cot for me near the fireplace. "Where you'll be warm, Tommy," he said.

I hadn't seen Scar and I asked, "Where is your dog, Mr. Williamson?"

And he replied, "He was killed by a grizzly we ran down. About a year ago it's been now. Buried him out back under an apple tree he liked to lay under when it got hot in the summer. I marked the spot with a cross."

"I marked Buddy's grave with a cross, too," I said. "We put flowers on his grave."

"I'm sorry about that, Tommy. I saw your cross back there, but I could never bring myself to say anything. I don't know why...I don't know why." And then he turned and slowly walked down the hall.

The next morning I awakened to the smell of bacon frying. Mother, Grandma and Jeanette were seated at a long picnic-type table, pancakes stacked before them topped with a fried egg and garnished with thick slices of ranch bacon. I hopped out of bed and over to the big wood-burning cast-iron stove where Mr. Williamson was frying sourdough pancakes on a large, black cast-iron griddle. There was a chill in the mountain air, and I reached out to the fire to warm myself. I watched him grease the griddle with a piece of bacon rind and pour dippers full of milky white sourdough onto it that puffed up to plate size pancakes. He handed me a stack with the bacon and egg and said, "See if you can wrap yourself around these, Tommy."

At the table was a bowl of raspberries from his garden for me and a blue enameled metal pitcher of thick cream to pour over them. "We have reached your father, and he is driving out from Spokane later today to pick us up," Mother announced when I sat down. "We'll be going back with him for a few days until the fires are under control, We still do not know whether the fire reached Luby Bay or not, but Mr Williamson thinks Jim Ward will stop it."

"Do you really think he can stop it?" I asked him.

He came over and put his hand on my shoulder and said, "If Jim Ward can't stop it, no one in this whole world can stop it. He's the best. I'd put money on it he'll tame that fire."

"Thank you Mr. Williamson," I said, near tears from loving Priest Lake and the cabin so.

Later that afternoon we heard Father's horn across the river from us. Mr. Williamson went over in one of his boats and brought him back. Father told of having encountered another fire a few miles out of Priest River. The fire had reached the road and smoke hung heavily in the air, and from to time he saw orange red spots of fire just off the road. Finally he was held back by fire fighters who said there were still sparks coming down on the road ahead.

A Forest Service truck came at last down-road from the burned over area. By that time there were cars backed up far behind Father, other anxious husbands. The driver of the truck said they had the fire under control, and he would lead them to safety beyond the burn.

Father moved us to Spokane. Jim Ward stopped the inferno with his backfire and saved Luby Bay. We returned to find Kalispel Bay devastated. The first day back we took a boat ride over to view the damage. Black snags stood straight and tall out of the blackened earth. In the great waste, a few pockets of green fire-resistant cedar survived where the ground was damp.   The shiny tracks of the Diamond Match narrow-gauge logging railroad snaked starkly up the valley of Kalispel Creek.   Along the bay a few fire-whitened stone fireplaces and twisted metal beds and cast-iron stoves was all that remained where once cabins stood.   When we turned our Elto Motor off, a quiet lay on the land.   There were no signs of life, not even a bird.

       We stopped at the Outlet over the years, when we were out for a ride in the Mary, to see Mr. Williamson.   He always offered us oatmeal cookies from a crockery cookie jar and chilled milk from a milk bottle he kept in a spring-fed, wooden trough at the back porch.   In the early days, the Indians had called him Chief Pawnee White Eagle because of his snow white hair.   He liked to have the children call him Pawnee Fred.

Epilogue

       The "Old Man Williamson" story first appeared in 1994 in "Kaniksu Stories of The Northwest."   In August of that year, I had a book signing in Bonners Ferry, a small town tucked away in the northeast corner of Idaho.   I was staying at my cabin in Luby Bay on Priest Lake at the time.   I drove over to Bonners Ferry, a distance of ninety miles, arriving at the bookstore around 8:30 in the morning.   The owner of the store and I set up a table and chairs near the front door.   I fanned out a number of books on the table and a sign promoting the signing.

       He offered me a cup of coffee which I gladly accepted.   We sat down to await the nine o'clock opening.   I mentioned that I had come there as a boy to fish the Moiey and Yak rivers with my father and that the fishing was great. He allowed how things had changed and that fishing was not what it used to be.   I said that the fishing was not what it used to be around Priest Lake.   Too many fishermen and so on.

       Promptly at 9:00 o'clock a man and two women bustled up to the door and marched across to the table.   They were nicely dressed, coats and hats.   I thought how nice it was to have people so eager to meet me.   The man was large.   I would judge around two twenty.

       "I'm Fred Williamson's nephew," he announced.

       I smiled and said, "I'm certainly pleased to meet you."

       "You called my uncle a white haired crusty old bastard in your book," he said, rather menacingly.

       I thought oh, oh watch out for that meaty right hand and replied, "Yes, I did."

       He hesitated, building the tension, and then said, "Well.   Your description of my uncle," pause, "fit him to a T."

He laughed and I laughed. He bought several books for friends and family, asked me to sign them, which I did, and left.

Moonlight on Priest Lake, Idaho.

SHE WHO SEES

A Myth

If you were to come to the Kaniksu, roam the mountain tops, feel their mysticism and magic, view the Pictured Rocks of the NoQuosh Kol, the ancient ones, walk the beaches of Lake Chal Qe Lee, and are fortunate to find an Indian arrowhead, you will forever dream of it and be drawn back.

And if you learn all you can about the ancient ones and walk a piece of their Silvis-Kaniksu Trail, the dreams will come to you just when you are between sleep and waking, and you will see her, She Who Sees, walking lightly down the Kaniksu Trail towards you. She will be beautiful in her long elkskin dress bleached almost white, her jet black hair pulled tightly back against her head and tied at the neck with a ribbon of leather and a shell amulet.

This day she had been to Chsawl cestkum, sacred mountain, where the sun ends the day and the most potent medicinal plants can be found. For she was a shaman, medicine woman, of great sumesh, or power. It was said she had the power over death.

She was returning to the No Quosh Kol summer encampment on Lake Chal Qe Lee. She had gathered a supply of roots, herbal teas, leafs of vine, clippings, plants with magical medicinal powers that grow in the alpine meadows and mountain tops. Now she hurried to be with her identical twin sons, White Eagle and White Owl and her husband Great Bear, chief of the No Quosh Kol.

The twins at birth were perfectly formed, identical in every way - an omen of great portent. Legends told of twins among the No Quosh Kol, but none so perfectly matched. It was of such magnitude as to bring great sumesh and honor to the No Quosh Kol.

She Who Sees smiled when she thought of the astonishment on Great Bear's face when he was first brought into the birthing chamber of the great lodge in the winter village on the ntxwe river. She had lain on a bed of soft furs and at either breast a babe had nestled.

"Two. Two identical boys," Great Bear had uttered in awe. "It brings great power to the No Quosh Kol, a blessing of the Guardian Spirits."

He had then touched each babe. As he did, he also offered a prayer to Amo'tken, He Who Sits on Top, creator of sky and mountain tops. Grandmother, Great Bear's mother, a peppery little woman, had then taken the twins to be bathed and dressed. He had knelt beside She Who Sees. He took her hand in his and brushed it with his lips. He placed around her neck a fetish of shells and turquoise stones that had come up the trade routes from far off places.

After he left, tears had welled up in her eyes and she felt the depth of his love. She was still young, only eighteen winters. Theirs had been a marriage of love, not one arranged with one from another Tribe as was often done for the first son of a chief. He was the seed of a long line of chieftains.

There had been days of feasting and gaming, and nights of dancing, singing and storytelling around great bonfires. Word had spread through the trade routes. Chieftains and medicine men from near and far had come to the celebrations. The greatest of them were awed and vied to be with the twins, to touch their garments, hoping to obtain sumesh. Though warned not to touch the babes themselves, many slyly managed to brush the cribs or soft furs that swathed them. Most of the emissaries showed open admiration and delight to be with the twins, but for a few the seeds of envy and avarice shown through.

II

Not seeing the twins on the beach when she arrived at camp, the old fear rose in She Who Sees throat. The fear that had been with her since that Vision Quest to Chsawl cestkum shortly after the twins birth when Owl had whispered the warning in her ear.

Theirs was the largest tule mat lodge at trails end. To either side other lodges showed among the tall orange bark pines. And out front beyond the white sandy beach, a knot of children splashed through the light green shore waters chasing schools of darting minnows. Many canoes, sharply pointed, like sturgeons, were pulled up on the beach, for every family had its own canoe.

Far out where the waters were deep purple, three islands appeared to float on the still, flat surface. Safe havens for canoes when the winds swept out of the mountains and the waves ran high. Beyond rose the granite peaks where the lightning danced in the night-time and the sun rose each morning. It was a land of mystery - a land of legends - legends passed down by storytellers from one generation to the next.

It was to Grandmother that She Who Sees turned to on her return. She looked within their lodge, and not finding her there, stepped across the carpet of pine needles laid down by the great pine trees and onto the open sunny white sands of the beach. There a knot of old men were playing their stick game and old women were sunning, cutting up softly tanned leather pelts and sewing them into moccasins. Racks stood in the bright sun with slabs of trout hung on them to dry. It was a busy time, one that She Who Sees loved best. It was a peaceful time, a family time, a happy time. It was a time of gathering and preparing foods for winter, in themselves soul satisfying ancient rites. She Who Sees loved to pick the 'sd SHAH' (wild huckleberries), and 'GAY t Khom' (strawberries), and to live in the open airy summer lodges, to lift her skirt and splash through the shallow waters with the children. And sometimes in secluded coves, she removed her clothes and swam out over the drop off, peered down into the crystal clear depths and watched trout drift by. Then ran up on a sandy beach and lay with the warm sands underneath her and the warm sun on her back, completely free, free of her many duties.

This day she slipped off her moccasins and waded ankle deep in the cool waters. They soothed and washed away the trail dust from her feet. At the north end of the beach was a large grey boulder, tall as a man. So large, only Amo'tken the creator himself could have placed it on the white sands. Grandmother often sat against its smooth warm surface on sunny days watching the children at play and sewing. She was there now.

Grandmother looked up expectantly as She Who Sees approached. Seeing the concerned look on her face and knowing the dark fear she bore said, "The twins have gone fishing with Great Bear and the younger men and women."

"Where did they go?" She Who Sees asked respectfully. Grandmothers were highly respected among the No Quosh Kol for their wisdom, wisdom handed down from one generation to the next.

"To the bay of Pictured Rocks. The cutthroat trout are running up the stream to spawn."

Relieved, She Who Sees dropped to the sand beside Grandmother, and leaned back against the great granite boulder. She ran her feet through the warm sand removing the last soreness of the long walk from Chsawl cestkum. She liked to watch Grandmother sew, her stitches so evenly spaced, uniform of size and straight of line.

"Perhaps," she mused, "She was overly concerned for the twins. It was many springs since her Vision Quest to Chsawl cestkum when Owl had issued the warning. It had been shortly after the twins' birth when they were at the ancestral village on the ntxwe..."what is it brings that frown to your forehead," Grandmother broke into her reverie.

"Oh, I was just thinking of Owl's warning. It still preys upon my thoughts."

"But that was so long ago. If anything were to come of it, surely it would have come long before now."

"I know. Yet I can't seem to rid myself of it."

"You've never really told me the whole story. Why don't you try."

"Well, it was at Great Bear's request that I made the Vision Quest. I carried no food for I fasted in order to cleanse my body, clear my spirit, and prepare myself to receive the visions and the words of my Guardian Spirits."

"How I savored the peace and quiet of the forest and release from the hubbub of the village. It then held several hundred people."

"I took to the Sylvis Trail, climbing swiftly, wanting to reach Chsawl cestkum before nightfall. I soon came to Sacred Meadow. Only a few pools remained to indicate it was once a large beaver pond. You've been there?"

"Yes, I've seen the tall old snags around its edge, the 's LATK ay' (sweathouse), felt the mystique. Is the 's LATK ay' still there?"

"Yes, it still stands. I found the frame solid, the bark and sod roof tight. But first I walked out to the lavender pools and offered a prayer to the spirits below."

"Ah...the bottomless lavender pools. So mysterious. You feel almost drawn into them."

She Who Sees nodded, "I built a fire over the pit of rocks within the lodge. When the coals died down, I raked them aside and poured water on the rocks. Steam rose, and I pulled a mat across the opening, removed my elk-skin dress and steeped in the steam until the sweat poured from my body. Then I walked carefully out over the quaking vegetal mat and plunged into an open pool. It was icy and I quickly climbed out."

Grandmother folded up her sewing and put it aside and then struggling, shifted into a more comfortable position.

"Grandmother, are you tiring?"

"No, no, Sees." Sees was grandmother's affectionate shortening of her name. She called her that when they were alone. "Go on, I want to hear the whole story."

"I repeated the ritual two times," she continued. "Three sweats, three baths as prescribed by the ancients. I felt the cleansing, the sharpening of my senses."

"After offering a prayer to the Guardian Spirits, I dressed and continued up the trail. Spring flowers covered the forest floor and their sweet scent filled the air. I tucked a few in my hair, and gathered a handful for the Guardian Spirits."

"Ah, spring flowers. One of life's treasures," grandmother murmered.

"The bald head of Chsawl cestkum and the trail slanting up its grassy side now loomed ahead. I came upon a clear rivulet that crossed the trail and drank deeply of its cold waters, it being the last I would encounter. The trees thinned out and I picked an armful of dry twigs for my evening fires."

"When finally I stepped out on top of Chsawl cestkum, the full sweep of its power and mysticism swept over me. I was driven to my knees. I laid the flowers on the ground and raised my arms in prayer to the Guardian Spirits to bless my quest."

"Weren't you alarmed, Sees?" Grandmother asked.

"I was, but then a feeling of peace and well being swept over me," she mused. Sees pulled herself back to the present.

"I remained on my knees in prayer. The sky that had been clear and blue early in the day now held great streamers of cloud. The sun was setting and lit them all colors of a rainbow. I rejoiced for such magnificence augured well for my quest."

"I gathered a few of the rocks from the stones scattered over the surface of Chsawl cestkum and placed them in a sacred circle. Within the circle I built a small fire with the twigs I had gathered on my way up. I took a handful of the powerful needles of a special pine, the last tree to grow on the mountain and threw them on the fire. Its aromatic scent filled the air, and the eternal winds carried the message of my presence to the Guardian Spirits."

"I did not eat nor sleep for four days and four nights and only left the mountain to get twigs for the fire and to drink from the spring."

"It was a long wait. Did you question the sense in staying on?" Grandmother asked.

"I did. My strength and patience were waning. I thought I would give it another day. And then shortly after midnight of the fifth day I heard the Owl and a vision filled the heavens. Riding the clouds were the twins,

67

one in the raiments of a chief and on his shoulder perched a bald eagle. At the waist of the other hung a medicine bag and on his shoulder perched a great snowy owl signifying a shaman of highest healing powers, and clairvoyance. I thought the one must be named White Eagle and the other White Owl."

"Then Owl, bearer of news, swept out of the dark and spoke to me."

"Beware of envy and malice," he intoned. "Beware of Amte'p and of those beyond the mountains from whence comes the sun."

"The whole northern sky then filled with lights that throbbed and grew and ebbed and slowly disappeared."

"When I returned to the village, I told Great Bear of my vision and the warning. I saw the concern rise in his eyes."

"The one twin who shall be shaman," I said "will be a blessing for all, yet the envy of some. His renown shall spread far and wide and people will come to him for healing. Yet, there may be some among them who under the spell of Amte'p, the evil one, may wish to do him harm. I felt this envy during the celebration of their birth. They must not be alone!"

"'We can't always be with them,'" he said to me. I agreed and then it was the thought came to me, a guardian - someone of great strength, a warrior, and I suggested it to him.

"'My brother Standing Bear, the tallest most powerful of my warriors—worth three ordinary braves.' he suggested. So it was Standing Bear came to live with us, and wherever the twins were he watched nearby."

She Who Sees concluded and then sat quietly, expectantly waiting for Grandmother to speak.

Grandmother sat for some time, her eyes half closed, deep in thought. She Who Sees wondered if she were asleep. Slowly Grandmother's eyes opened and she spoke softly, thoughtfully, "In their early years it was you and I who taught them the ways of the No Quosh Kol. Our way of life was idyllic. There was always danger, but we taught them always to be on guard. There are the she bear with cubs, the ntxwe river's currents and rapids, fire, lightning, strangers, especially strangers - the plots of Amte'p, and enemy medicine men."

"Great Bear and Standing Bear taught them the ways of the warrior, of bravery, skill with the atlatl. They can split a wand or drive a dart through the enemy at great distance. They are in their fourteenth summer, no longer children. Soon they go on Vision Quest and will return men. Take wives. They stand taller than most men. They have great sumesh. There will always be danger, and they will meet it alone even as we have."

She Who Sees didn't speak immediately, her eyes fastened wistfully on the distant islands as if contemplating other times. When she turned to grandmother, it was with a determined look, "Yes, grandmother, they are well prepared to meet the future, whatever Amo'tken and Amte'p have in store for them. It is time to let go."

Grandmother nodded, then straightened abruptly, gesturing towards the point, "Look Sees, the fishermen return!"

She Who Sees turned just in time to see the first canoe rounding the point. It rode low in the water, heavily loaded with fish. It moved swiftly with White Owl and White Eagle at the paddles.

White Owl was the one in front, the laughing, lighthearted, daring one, savoring the excitement of the moment. White Eagle knelt on his heels at the stern, calm, controlled, collected. A smile played across the lips of She Who Sees and she thought, "Look alikes yet so different underneath...the only way to tell them apart."

They beached the canoe and She Who Sees and Grandmother moved down to meet them. They were soon joined by the rest of the fishing fleet led by Great Bear and Standing Bear.

III

She Who Sees stepped up to one of the canoes, looked in and gasped, "The fish...so huge...so many!"

"Best in years," Great Bear enthused. "The big ones are char."

"So big their tails touched the ground when slung over our backs," White Eagle cut in, still keyed up over the grand excitement of the day.

A clamoring clutch of men, women and children now pressed around the fishermen straining to hear their every word. Great Bear reached into a canoe and pulled out a char slab and holding it with both hands thrust it overhead. He stood an imposing head taller than the onlookers. Around his neck he wore a string of grizzly bear claws and in his black hair three white tipped eagle feathers symbol of his status as chief of all the lower No Quosh Kols.

A bubble of "ohs" and "ahs" rose from the crowd.

"Yes, a char, mean devils," he confirmed a perky little woman's question. She nodded knowingly to her friends. "But let me tell you about the cutthroat!"

"There were hoards of them," his voice rising, "swarming over the shoals at the mouth of the stream when we pulled in this morning. So big their backs protruded out of the water."

"We beached the canoes and walked up along the stream. Fish filled the stream from bank to bank. It seemed like we could walk across on their backs."

"A short way upstream where the water deepens and the stream bed is flat and gravelly," Great Bear continued, "I chose to put the weir and traps."

"We anchored a trap at either side of the stream, piled brush in between and weighted it down with the stones," he further explained. The little boys listened raptly, in quiet awe. "Now the fish, their upward movement shut off, had no where to go but into the traps."

"Immediately," Great Bear exclaimed, betraying excitement, "the baskets started filling. And the size of them! As long as my arm! We'd hardly gotten out of the water when we had to jump back in."

"We seized the trap and thrust it back into the gap in the weir. The other trap we emptied further back from the stream bank and quickly returned it before too many fish got through."

"Then disaster hit!" he exclaimed, his voice rising in fervor. "Huge char came in over the shoals. They came like evil wraths from Amte'p determined to feast on cutthroat spawn!"

"I grasped a spear and sprinted downstream closely followed by White Eagle and White Owl. The demons had to be stopped before they destroyed the weir."

"I splashed out into the waters—into the wild thrashing surging giant fish. Raised my spear! Thrust it down! The sharp points sliced through a huge fish impaling it to the bottom!"

"The fish writhed mightily to break free, but I clubbed it behind the head and pitched it up on the bank."

"I speared another and whirling around threw it up on the bank."

"Fish were surging past me, but now White Owl and White Eagle were in the stream above me attacking the great fish."

"When it was all over, fourteen of the monstrous fish lay stretched out on the banks," Great Bear recounted, his eyes gleaming. "The waters of the stream ran red. We were bloodied and wet."

"By early afternoon we had caught and filleted all the fish the canoes could carry safely."

"We removed the baskets from the weir and submerged them in the lake waters where the raccoons and other scavengers couldn't get at them."

"There was little free board showing when we pulled away from the beach. As we looked back, the ravens had moved in, and bold jays darted in and out snatching their share of the spoils."

IV

A full moon had risen through the saddle in the mountains across Lake Chal Qe Lee casting a trail of light across its waters that led up to the cooking fires burning brightly along shore at the encampment. Cutthroat and grouse broiled on spits set over the fires. On flat topped cedar log tables were spread 'sPOT ka', roast camas mixed with black lichen, and birch bark baskets of "GAY t Khom', strawberries. There was tea made from the leafs of a vine that grew at high elevations. The air was filled with the aroma from green pine branches that were thrown on the fires from time to time.

Great Bear took the first cutthroat to turn golden brown to She Who Sees. She held the spitted fish up to the moon and offered a prayer of thanks to the moon spirit for the bounty of the harvest and thanks to the fish for giving of itself to her. Great Bear then took fish for himself. White Owl and White Eagle drifted off to eat by themselves.

"It is a happy time," She Who Sees murmured.

"The best of times," he agreed for he loved this jewel of a lake and the tall mountains across the way that he had ranged freely as a youth. The cares of ruling the village on the ntxwe were far removed. Here his people were happy. Only after he and She Who Sees had found a place to sit did the elders and rest help themselves to the feast. After a long winter of eating dried food, the fresh caught fish and berries tasted good, spirits rose and soon it was a boisterous, happy crowd. They ate and then they drifted off to a large bonfire. The flames danced, highlighting the faces of the onlookers. Large white pine cones were roasted over the fire to release the pine nuts which people cracked and nibbled on.

When the bonfire died down, Great Bear turned to Grandmother and said, "Tell us a story."

She was a storyteller, and when she rose and moved beside the fire a hush fell over the crowd. "For the grownups or the children?" she asked.

"For the children," Great Bear replied.

"Would you like to hear the story of jaybird, chipmunk, or coyote? Or how about mosquito," she asked, a twinkle in her eyes, knowing full well that the children liked frightening stories.

"Mosquito," the children chorused, scarcely able to contain themselves.

"Well," Grandmother said, pausing long enough to build the suspense. "This is a story my grandmother told me. It happened long ago when animals could talk. There lived a mosquito who had many brothers. They were mean, very mean. They had a fight with their enemies, and all were killed except for Mosquito. He escaped and hid in a sweat lodge."

"So the enemy speared the sweat lodge with their long spears, barely missing Mosquito. He grabbed the blade of one of the spears and jiggled it back and forth with his nose and made his nose bleed. He then smeared the spear with his blood. When the enemy pulled the spear out, they said, "Well, mosquito is dead. We can go now."

"Mosquito stayed in the sweat lodge until morning and then he left. He saw that all his brothers were dead and became very angry. He swore he would kill four villages of people before he was satisfied."

"When he got to the first village, all people had left, they were so afraid of Mosquito. Mosquito landed and speared their tracks and all the people died."

"He went to another village and the same thing happened. The people all ran away, and all died when he speared their tracks."

"At the third village he was invited for soup of camas and berries, but he was not hungry. He wanted revenge. He speared all of their tracks except for one. He could not find his tracks. He was a boy. He ran to the next village and warned the people that Mosquito was coming, "to kill everyone."

Grandmother paused as though she couldn't think of what to say next.

"The blood soup. The blood soup." The children chimed in.

"Oh, yes. The blood." Grandmother teased. "By this time Mosquito was very hungry. An old woman at the next village made some soup of blood and waited for Mosquito to come. When he arrived, Old Woman invited him to come in and told him she had some blood soup. Being so hungry he agreed to have some."

"She set the pot in front of him and offered him a spoon. He shoved it aside and announced 'I have my own soup spoon.' He removed it from his head where he carried it stuck in his hair."

"When he finished that pot full of blood, Old Woman had another pot ready. While he was enjoying this pot of soup, an idea came to Old Woman. And while he was having a third pot of soup, she told the young children of the camp to push Mosquito's canoe out into the river and let it float away. By now, Mosquito was very full of blood and could not move."

Old Woman said, 'Your canoe has floated away.'

'Tell the children to get my canoe,' he ordered.

'They don't know how to swim,' Old Woman replied.

"Mosquito jumped into the river to try to get his canoe. Old Woman told the children, 'Hurry and gather pine needles.' They did. Then she told them, 'Hurry throw them in the water.' All the needles started floating towards Mosquito."

"He begged for help. Then one of the pine needles poked him and he burst."

Old woman said, 'Now you are destroyed. When all animals turn into real people, you are going to become a pest still bothering to get what blood you can carry. You will still be Mosquito but in a different form.'

The children clasped their hands together and hopped about in delight and asked for more. But Grandmother said, "It's bedtime. Off to bed."

Great Bear ordered dried pine branches filled with pitch be thrown on the dying embers. They crackled and spit sparks and flames that flew up into the black of night.

Drummers picked up a slow beat on their drums gradually raising it to a feverish pitch that reached into the souls of the onlookers. Dancers rose and circled the fire in ritualistic steps handed down over the millennia. From time to time they sang their medicine songs, songs that told of personal triumphs and brave deeds. They danced to exhaustion, and their places were soon taken up by others. Bats, attracted by the flames, flitted in and out of the blackness and owls spoke. They danced until sky lightened behind Twin Peaks.

V

For White Owl and White Eagle there was a new excitement in the air. They had overheard She Who Sees and Great Bear talking of Vision Quests. "They should go together," She Who Sees said with conviction.

"No," Great Bear said, "A boy goes alone and he returns a man. Each must seek his own Guardian Spirit, his way of life. It has always been that way. It is tradition."

"But the omen," She Who Sees pleaded. "The warning of the Owl."

"They're both big, strong. They are fast and sure with the atlatl. They run like deer. One will return to become a great chief. The other to be a great medicine man. They will soon take wives. These things will separate them."

"I feel danger in the air. I have for some time." She Who Sees retorted.

"There is always danger," Great Bear said. "We cannot live in fear. Fear is the greatest enemy. They must learn to meet with fear and danger, She Who Sees. The sooner they go on Vision Quest the better. Speak to them."

Perhaps it is only the old fear, my imagination, She Who Sees thought as she looked for the twins. I must not let them know. Best they have no fear. They must be somewhere near camp. They wouldn't have wandered off too far. She found them with their uncle making flint points for atlatl darts and spears. It was an art that fascinated her. When she arrived, they had just removed chips of agate and flint from a heat treating pit where they had "cooked" for twenty four hours to make them more workable. She watched quietly for sometime as they used their hammer stones, smooth water worn rock, to roughly shape the chips. They first removed large flakes leaving a rough wavy edge all the way around the chip. They then straightened the edges and thinned the piece by removing bumps and ridges. With a short thick piece of antler, ground to an angle at one end, they further thinned the piece and straightened the edges. Then, using a smaller piece of antler and light blows, notched the point and gave it a keen cutting edge. The points were then attached to atlatl darts with moist animal sinew which shrinks and hardens as it dries securing the point rigidly in place.

"Was there anything you wanted?" Standing Bear asked having sensed that She Who Sees had not come just to watch them make flint points.

"Yes, there is something I wanted to talk to you about," she confessed. "Vision Quests."

"The twins?" Standing Bear asked.

"Yes."

White Eagle and White Owl, in mounting excitement, asked, "When can we go?"

"Would you rather speak to the twins alone?" Standing Bear broke in.

"No. I need your counsel." Then turning to the twins said seriously but with warmth, "It will be a few days before you can start your Vision Quests. There are rites to be performed first - sweat baths, bathing in cold running water, periods of praying to the Guardian Spirits."

"This will be the most important quest you shall ever make," she continued. "You search for your Guardian Spirits. Guardian Spirits are the source of power and wisdom."

"Your Guardian Spirit will place great demands on you. You must obey or you will suffer great torments. The Guardian Spirits work in ways you may not always understand, but they will be there always to guard you from evil spirits."

"Do you have a Guardian Spirit?" White owl, his brows furrowed, asked.

"Yes, I do," Sees nodded. "The Guardian Spirit came to me. Girls do not seek a Guardian." Then went on, "During your quest you may receive one or more Medicine Songs. These will sustain you in difficult times. And you sing them at the mid-winter Medicine Dance and other important ceremonies."

"You will make a circuit of five peaks, peaks haunted by the Guardian Spirits. You build a sacred circle of rocks and within it a sacred fire. Place a branch of the mountain pine on it to alert the Spirits of your presence. Eat no food. Stay awake. Listen, meditate, and watch. The

Guardian Spirit may come to you in a vision or perhaps send Owl with a message."

"This is the rite of manhood. You go alone, and return a man."

"You both are strong. Have no fear."

"Can I go to cee cee Ah and Chsawl cestkum and No Quosh Kol and Baldy and No Quosh Kol Rock?" White Eagle put in eagerly.

"And I want to go to Notch Lake, Nob Mountain, Notch Mountain and Twin Peaks and Sentinel Rock," White Owl added quickly.

"I see you have been thinking about this," She Who Sees said, the fear rising, anyplace but the mountains of the rising sun.

Before she could answer Standing Bear interjected, "They have each ranged over those mountains, hunted there. They know them better than anyone. Those to the east are the highest, closest to Amo'tken and the Guardian Spirits. Ideal for he who would be Shaman."

Oh if only he knew my dread of the east, She Who Sees thought. He forgets the warning of Owl, it was so long ago. But I can't let them see my concern and she said, "Then it is settled. The next two days will be devoted to the sweat baths, the prayers, and meditation. And the next day you will go on Vision Quest."

VI

The mountains across Lake Chal Qe Lee were still dark and the stars, just gave way to First Light, when White Owl stepped into a canoe and pushed out on the flat shore waters. He carried no food. He would fast. His weapons were left behind, only the flint knife in its sheath on his thigh was he permitted to take with him. The quest was a sacred journey to be approached in a deeply religious manner.

White Eagle had stepped onto the Sylvis Trail at the same time that White Owl stepped into the canoe. He, too, carried no weapons, only the sheath knife for cutting bark and shavings to start a sacred fire that would announce his presence to the Guardian Spirits.

White Owl dug deeply with his paddle, and the canoe leapt forward. The canoe of the No Quosh Kol was sturdy, yet light, built for speed. It was only two hands deep yet it was seaworthy. The sturgeon shaped bow knifed through the wind. The No Quosh Kol were renowned for their skills with the bark canoe.

He cut across to No Quosh Kol Island and hugged its south shore. The lonesome cry of the loon drifted across the water, heightening the feeling of loneliness he had felt since leaving the encampment. He had never been alone before, never separated from White Eagle. They were so close that when one felt pain, the other felt pain too.

75

THOMAS F. LACY

When he came to the open water beyond No Quosh Kol Island, the wind had risen, and there was a ripple on the water. He increased the cadence of his strokes for the winds in this mountainous country could pick up and start savage waves to rolling. Stroke - stroke - stroke, faster and faster. Up at the narrows he could see the waves building, their caps white. Before long the waves around him were rolling higher and higher, and he had to quarter across them. It was difficult to keep in line with the little cove where he would beach the canoe and where the trail started that would take him to the crest of the mountains.

Spray was breaking over his bow now as he went up and over a wave and into its trough. Water was gathering in the bottom of the canoe. He could run with the waves, but that would take him far off course. He was enjoying the challenge, the thrill of fighting the wind and the wild waves, beating the spirits of Lake Chal Qe Lee. He drove the canoe up a wave and steadied it with the flat of the paddle as he rode down the other side. He felt the surging power in his arms and his legs. He roared back at the wind. He knew he would win. Little by little the wind spirit gave in as he drew closer and closer to shore, and then he was swooping in to the shelter of the cove. He turned, waved his paddle at the waves and shouted his defiance to the spirit of the wind.

He pulled the canoe up on the beach, lifted it to his shoulders, and strode up into the forest. He placed it in a thick copse of fir whose drooping branches hid it.

A stream entered the cove. It came from Notch Lake, a small alpine lake that lay in a cirque at the base of Notch Mountain. It was not a large stream. It was a fast stream, a joyous stream that made music. Along its north bank a trail ran that led to the saddle between Notch Mountain and Twin Peaks.

The day was warming, the sky blue through the tall trees with a few clouds passing overhead when White Owl stepped on the trail. At first the trail wound through giant cedars, the ground carpeted with green moss and scattered tall ferns. It followed the stream closely for some time coming to a falls, a falls high enough to impede the runs of whitefish and cutthroat. Little sun filtered through the dense canopy overhead.

But then the trail left the valley floor and angled upwards through an open forest of tall orange bark pine trees. Here the forest floor was carpeted with their brown needles and sprinkled with their pine cones. The soil was poor, dry and undergrowth sparse. The sun beat down and his mouth grew parched, but nothing could dampen the exhilaration he felt. He had hunted the black tailed deer and bear here, and higher up the mountain goats with his uncle and White Eagle. And now, though he missed White

76

Eagle, he experienced the thrill and deep satisfaction of accomplishing the Vision Quest on his own.

From time to time he would come to a promontory where he could see the flash of the stream far below and to the west stretches of Lake Chal Qe Lee growing smaller and smaller. Ahead Notch Mountain loomed high above.

Before long the trail leveled off, caught up to the stream and crossed over to the other side. Here the forest was of dark green fir and some cedar. The stream became smaller and smaller and soon divided. The trail followed the left branch up to the saddle in the mountains. The other branch tumbled down the mountain from Notch Lake. There was no trail along this branch, but the terrain was more open here, the trees fewer, the forest floor carpeted with bear grass now in bloom, its white snowball flowers dotting the landscape.

The trail was now behind him, no sign of human passage. The terrain grew steeper. As he climbed, the words of She Who Sees swept through his mind, "The most important vision quest you will ever make - your Guardian Spirit will place great demands upon you - you must obey - Guardian Spirits are the source of power and wisdom." It had all been overwhelming, somewhat fearful. Yet he was eager to meet his Guardian Spirit, and he pushed ahead rapidly.

He paused once to scoop up a handful of water from the little stream for the sun was now hot and heavy. Once he came to a talus slope, large granite blocks, that he had to pick his way over, leaping from boulder to boulder. But that, too, was thrilling. And then abruptly, the timber ended, and in front of him lay Notch Lake. It was surrounded on three sides by steep talus slopes interspersed with sheer granite walls. Gaggles of pine had taken root in hollows and occasional ravines that led to the top. At the far end a small patch of green grass showed where a little stream entered the lake. A line of dwarf pines indicated its course up the steep wall behind.

White Owl made his way around the little lake to the grassy area. Beyond the grass stood a copse of pine. Its floor was covered with fallen pine needles. Here White Owl made his camp. He cleared the needles from a small area and built a circle of stones. He gathered dead branches and placed them in the circle for a fire.

Then he scrambled back to a large slab of granite that sloped out into the water. He climbed onto it, stripped off his deerskin garments, then sat down, his arms outstretched behind him. A feeling of loneliness swept over him, mixed with doubt, uncertainty. He ran his hand over the smooth surface of the stone, felt a warmth and power emanating from it.

He stood and looked down into the deep blue waters. He took a deep breath, prayed that his Guardian Spirit would reveal itself to him and plunged in. The waters were icy from snow melt, shocking, numbing and he felt pulled down, down and then catapulted upwards. He shot out of the waters and clambered onto the warm comforting surface of the great stone.

He dressed and returned to his camp. It was turning cool and soon the coldness of an alpine night would be upon him. With his flint knife he whittled a handful of shavings from a weathered stick heavy with pitch and lit it with sparks from two fire flints struck together. In the depths of the valley, it was turning dark. Only the peak of Notch Mountain reflected the rays of a setting sun. He felt the hunger pains, but the good side of that was they'd help keep him awake this first night.

And well it was for from the moment his canoe turned into the cove that morning he was being watched. A small band of Ravens, Indians from lands of the rising sun, had been with him, watching his movements. Yet his intuitive powers of foresight had not warned him.

He stayed awake all this first night, and though he prayed often the Guardian Spirits did not make themselves known to him nor did Owl speak to him. He rose with first light, quenched the remains of his fire in the waters of the lake and buried them. Then he returned the circle of rocks to their original places and spread needles on the ground. The campsite would soon show no sign that someone had passed that way.

The climbing was harder, the terrain steeper than the day before. He followed close on the stream up and up. It became but a trickle of water that over time had worn a cut in the valley wall. There were stout scrub bushes firmly anchored in the crevices and the occasional dwarf tree to grasp and winch himself up. At last the flow of water disappeared in a crevice. From there a steep talus slope lay ahead over which he clambered, finally topping out in a small saddle.

On his left rose the rocky shoulder of Notch Mountain and on his right a head wall that led to Nob Mountain. Ahead was a small alpine meadow with a shallow pond in its center. It was lush with grass and bordered with dwarf pine and fir.

At the far end of the meadow the land sloped upwards. He stepped out into the meadow and as he did a brood of blue grouse took off, set its wings and sailed off down the mountainside to a neighboring ridge.

He circled the pond, mounted the rise of land and looked about him for a way to Nob Peak. Ahead and below was a blue alpine lake and beyond was a ridge that ran up to Nob Peak. But it was a long way down and a long way up.

A flash of white to his right caught his eye. "Ah, 'le no MTO', White Ghost of the high country, it with the black stiletto horns and white beard. It would know the shortest route to the top of the Nob Peak head wall."

As he watched, le no MTO moved slowly, carefully up the head wall, zigging and zagging, disappearing and re-appearing as if endowed with magical powers. Finally it reached the sky line, looked back as if to say, "That's how you do it." Then it turned and was gone.

White Owl moved up to where he had first seen 'le no MTO.' A series of ledges led upwards. He followed coming shortly to a crease in the wall. On the floor he could see le-no-MTO's tracks leading upwards. "Here is where White Ghost had temporarily disappeared," he surmised. He moved up the crease and soon stood on top of the crest of the head wall.

But for a few low growing junipers, the top of the head wall was bare and no more than a step or two wide. The juniper had some medicinal uses, some sacred qualities, and he plucked a few sprigs and placed them in his medicine bag. The footing was granular decayed stone, sure, smooth as a wind swept sandy beach. It was early in the day and no need to hurry, the rounded rise of Nob Peak now showing clearly ahead. He looked into alpine meadows tucked into the heads of draws that ran off the mountain. In one he saw le-no-MTO not far below on a naked ridge watching him. Below it were several nannies with kids.

It was another blue sky day, windy but warm - good to be walking along the top of the land, the sun shining down out of a clear sky. From time to time he felt as though there were eyes upon him but passed it off as loneliness and the haunting mysticism of high country.

He dawdled. No one to urge him on, to make something of the day. He glanced back taking in the whole range of mountains to their disappearance in the north. There was Notch Mountain. He measured its height against the others - the tallest of all. It would be a morning's work climbing its south shoulder, searching for handholds, pulling his weight up and over skin scratching ragged stone.

Beyond lay Twin Peaks, a relatively easy climb; down Notch Mountain's north shoulder, through the saddle and up to the highest of the two peaks. This side, at least what he could see of it, was bald, a few spikes of small trees showing on its grassy slope, the top itself bare granite so light in color that at a distance it could be taken for snow.

He watched a hawk ride the thermals searching for rock conies and other small creatures that inhabited the harsh landscape, it being a poor way of making a living, he thought. He sang his medicine song as he moved slowly along.

The top of Nob Mountain, which at a distance had appeared rounded, he found to be flat and on its surface was a sacred circle of fire blackened stones, evidence of former Vision seekers. And off to one side stood a cairn of stones, high as his shoulders. White Owl found a flat stone, scratched the outline of an owl on it and placed it on the cairn.

To the east he noted an enormous void and peered over its edge. There was a sheer drop of a thousand stomach churning feet. He drew back quickly but not before seeing in a basin to the left, a small turquoise blue lake, and in another basin off to the right a red lake. Amo'tken himself must have colored the lakes he thought. They would be of momentous religious portent. There was a ridge between them that sloped out from Nob Mountain. Some day, he promised himself, he would climb down to them.

Below him to the west he could see dwarf pine trees and an opening green with grass indicating a spring where he might quench his thirst. He scrambled down and found a flow of water, and scooped it up in his cupped hands. On the way back he gathered dry branches for a fire and a green branch of the pine to place on the fire announcing his presence to the Guardian Spirits.

That night his fire shone like a star perched on the mountain top. She Who Sees had waited anxiously from first darkness for it, and having seen it offered a prayer of gratitude to the Guardian Spirits. Yet she could not shake an ominous feeling, a feeling that Amte'p the evil one was plotting trouble. Several times during the night she slipped out of bed and down to the beach. Each time the fire burned and she knew White Owl still was safe.

Again White Owl stayed awake throughout the night, but his head dropped briefly a few times to his chest. Black Hawk, leader of the band of Ravens, smiled at his warriors. "It won't be long. Another night he'll fall asleep and we need no longer fear his great powers."

The hunger pains in his stomach turned his thought from celestial to camas cakes filled with nuts and berries, just caught cutthroat sizzling on a spit over a fire, foam berries beaten into a tasty pleasing froth. Then hurriedly, to appease the Guardian Spirits for these transgressions, cleared his mind of such sinful thoughts with prayer and meditation. Yet the sun rose without the Guardian Spirit, revealing itself.

He let the fire die down and when the embers no longer smoldered nor felt warm to the touch, headed back down the ridge top. As he walked he studied Notch Mountain. Others before had always climbed it from the saddle on the north side, a gentler approach. It appeared if he could climb the early part the rest would not be that difficult. Otherwise he'd have to go back down to Notch Lake, on to the trade route and up to the saddle. "Too long," he said to himself. "I'll chance it. I'll try the shorter route upward over Notch Mountain."

He walked the ridge, down the head wall to the meadow, around the pond and up the slope to the saddle. He took one last look down at Notch Lake and then a long final appraising look at the bulk of Notch Mountain.

The east and west slopes were impregnable, the only approach being the barren rocky south shoulder.

First there was a near vertical stretch of large slabs and chunks of granite to clamber over, split off the granite shoulder of Notch Mountain by winter freezing and spring thaws over the millennia. Then there was a sheer rock wall to climb followed by a smooth granite slide, which if he ever started sliding down, he would not stop until he was dashed on the wicked boulders below. Once into it he couldn't turn around.

The boulders were of a size he had to reach up and pull himself over, sometimes wedge a foot between two boulders to gain a step and then pull himself up. It was harsh going over the abrasive rock, punishing. The air was thin and with the heavy exertion his breathing was labored and his lungs burned. He had to stop from time to time 'til the burning passed and then go on.

By mid-morning he'd come to the sheer wall, his palms scratched, showing the abrasive clasp of the granite, the sweat pouring out staining his deerskin shirt. The fissure in the wall, as seen in the distance, assuring a means to climb it, did not run its full length. In fact he could not reach it. And then as though the means had been placed there the thought came to him, "Build a platform of stone against the wall."

He piled stones, choosing only the flattest, until he could get a toehold in the fissure. And then he reached overhead, placed each hand into the fissure, applied pressure, palms to fissure. Then he tentatively lifted his right foot and pressed the toe into the fissure above the other foot. Ah, he was firmly anchored above the stone pile. Then he reached gingerly, moving left hand ahead of the right. It held. Then a foot above the other. It was working. Hand over hand, foot over foot he worked his way up the sheer wall. Like a fly he hugged its smooth surface and then he felt it change under him from sheer wall to slick slide slanting upwards. Soon he was moving on hands and knees, then on foot cautiously, a misstep on the polished surface, and he would slide over the edge onto the rocks now far below. Ahead he could see boulders and soon he was among them, and he rested in their safe embrace. For the first time since he started the climb he looked about him. Nob Mountain was far below him and looked like a knife with an aberration at one end. The lake below it looked like a turquoise stone he could hold in his hand, and the climb below him a slide to the underworld. He thought the day was beautiful, and life wonderful, and he was lucky to be here and breathing.

The marvel of the climb had not gone unnoticed. Black Hawk and his men observed the whole thing from the ridge above Notch Lake near the saddle and they were impressed. Awed would describe it better. Cowed better yet. There was no way they could follow in broad daylight. They'd

81

be seen on the bare rocks, even if they could negotiate the sheer wall and rock slide. And after dark it would be impossible. He couldn't risk it, but how could he face the wrath of Thunder Raven, chief of the Ravens. Better to end it all here than there.

Then it came to him. White Owl would be on Vision Quest five nights. This would be but the third. Surely White Owl would not go back. He would go down the north shoulder of Notch Mountain to the saddle, and what more likely place for his fourth night than Twin Peaks, easily accessible and sacred, if rumors were true, sacred to the No Quosh Kol.

They'd drop down to Notch Lake, follow the outlet stream to the trade route, and lay in wait for White Owl at the saddle. But what if White Owl should go the other way? Ah! He'd leave a scout behind.

After a brief rest, White Owl continued up Notch Mountain, leaping animatedly from boulder to boulder. Soon he stepped out onto the south rim of the notch. As far as he could see in the four directions, none were so tall. None bore such a notch. He thought, "The creator, Amo'tek himself, must have cut it out." And his spirits soared. "This must be the home of the Guardian Spirits, and surely tonight I shall meet mine."

In the bottom of the notch was a level area, the accumulation of the dust of time and the workings of winter freeze and spring thaws. The heat from his sacred fire would be reflected off the granite walls and keep him warm. But first he must find firewood and water. He had not had a drink since early in the morning, and now it was well into the afternoon, and he was thirsty.

There would be water in the saddle between Notch Mountain and Twin Peaks. He moved off down the ridge top. The walking was easy, the slope gentler than that of the morning. The surface was granite and gravel with the occasional large boulders to clamber over. Just before he reached the saddle, he came upon a sheer drop of a hundred feet or more. At its base in the saddle was a pond of clear water, a watering hole for the mountain goats that ranged the mountain crest. The shoulders sloped gently away from the cliff and he was able to detour around it. As he came up to the pond he saw fresh tracks of the mountain goats in the soft soil. He dropped to his knees and drank deeply from the sweet water.

He lingered by the pond, the damp soil cool to his feet, its softness a blessing after the hard sharp granite slopes of Notch Mountain. He discovered a patch of 'xas xas,' an aromatic root, a medicine, in the damp soil. He harvested a few roots and put them in his medicine bag.

There were trees in the saddle, short stout pine trees and the occasional snag, storm polished, smooth, gray. Like ghosts, they loomed above the dark green forest. There was a haunted mystic aura about them and White Owl felt their power, their great sumesh. He circled one with his arms and pressed his body against it as he had been taught by Grandmother. He offered up a prayer of supplication to the Guardian Spirits for power to sustain him the remaining days of his quest.

The ground was littered with the dead branches of tree and snag torn off by winters winds. He laid up two piles and bound them into two bundles with leather thongs, took a last drink from the pond, lifted the bundles to his shoulders, skirted the cliff, returning to the ridge top.

He arrived at the notch as the sun disappeared in an orange sky to the west beyond Lake Chal Qe Lee and the now black wall of mountains on the horizon. He hastened to form a sacred circle of stones and to start a fire against the cold of another alpine night.

At the No Quosh Kol camping ground on Lake Chal Qe Lee, She Who Sees having watched since dusk and now seeing the tiny point of light, smiled at Great Bear who watched with her, "He's safe for another day."

"Yes, and you should not worry. White Owl can take care of himself."

Once during the night White Owl, in a dream, was suddenly bathed in brightness, a glow of love and warmth and then he saw She Who Sees smiling, beckoning, and heard the words, "Come home." He tried to reach out to her but dreamed his hands were tied behind his back. Then all he could see was the blackness. He waited, but she did not return.

He awakened. The fire had burned out. It had all been more of a feeling than a seeing. He wondered, "could it have been a dream or was it a vision and a warning? Should he flee the mountain or should he follow his quest the two remaining days?"

The next day in bright daylight he was more inclined to believe it was a dream and hurried down to the saddle. Once again he felt eyes upon him and wondered if he shouldn't take the trail back to Lake Chal Qe Lee. But then he saw the ghostly snags and felt the eeriness of the place and shrugged off the feelings of eyes as part of its aura. He knew if he got a step ahead of anyone they could never catch up to him. He had faith in his physical powers and yet did not fully comprehend his powers of foresight. Besides, he had often felt eyes upon him only to discover it was a partially hidden animal - deer, caribou, moose. Here, it was probably a mountain goat.

The south slope of Twin Peaks was grassy with a sprinkling of trees scattered over its bare surface. The walking was fine and easy. The sky was partly cloudy, the sun peeping in and out of the blue spots. The last part was rocky and on top the twin peaks were jagged upthrusts of granite and a jumble of boulders. He topped out on the lower of the two peaks. He was pleased to see a sacred fire pit and a cairn of stones built up, high as his waist. He was not the first to seek his Vision here.

He could see to the limits of the world. Lake Chal Qe Lee - most of it - lay at his feet and wherever he looked were wave upon wave of mountains. The other side of Twin Peaks fell straight away to a vast field of ragged rocks. Beyond rose the massive form of Sentinel Rock, taller than the tallest tree, a wonder to view, most sacred and site for the last night of his Vision Quest.

That night he built a large fire in the sacred fire pit. The flames leaping high were seen by She Who Sees who had been watching anxiously on the beach and now returned to her lodge.

White Owl offered a prayer to the Guardian Spirits and to Amo'tken. He had now gone without sleep for three nights and he struggled to keep awake, but soon his head fell to his chest then bobbed up. Startled, he looked about, tried to keep his eyes open, but slowly drifted off.

Black Hawk and his men had slept most of the day and were refreshed. They watched nearby and when he no longer moved slipped into the circle of firelight. Then as one they pounced on White Owl, wrenched his arms behind him and tied them together with a leather thong. White Owl lashed out with his feet, dug into the bellies and crotches of his attackers with his elbows and knees, struggled to his feet, only to have Black Hawk drop a noose over his head and with a deft jerk shut off his wind bringing him to bay as he would a wild animal.

White Owl, his eyes flashing, enraged, shouted, "You have broken the sacred Vision Quest. Damn your souls. May Amo'tek wreak vengeance on you."

All but one of the warriors were cowed, but he, a hot headed young brave, snatched a long bladed flint knife from his thigh sheath and shouting "For Amte'p" leaped at White Owl. Black Hawk stepped in sweeping up a stone and crushed his skull. Blood spilled over the ground.

"Fool," Black Hawk muttered, "Thunder Raven ordered us to bring him back unharmed."

Thunder Raven, chief of the Ravens, a bull of a man who ruled by fear had sternly warned Black Hawk, "I want White Owl alive. Alive he will bring great power. Power to wage war against our enemies and win back our ancestral lands."

Black Hawk surveyed the blood, the body clearly pointing to who had been there and where to look for White Owl. Then he noticed that White Owl and the dead warrior were of like size. And then he thought, "Switch their buckskin garments and make it look like a grizzly attack."

They bloodied the victim's buckskin, ripped it, lacerated the skin as though done by a powerful swipe of a grizzly's paw. The face, unrecognizable, appeared to be bashed in by another swipe of the maddened brute. And as a final touch, a telling touch, Black Hawk tied the two owl feathers from White Owl's head into the hair of the victim. Then they left keeping to the rocky east slope of the mountain leaving no sign of their passing.

At the moment that Black Hawk had crushed the hot headed warrior's skull, She Who Sees rose bolt upright from her bed of skins, an anguished cry bursting from her lips. She grasped Great Bear's arm. "Great Bear, Great Bear! It's White Owl. He is in terrible danger."

Great Bear, coming out of a deep sleep, scarcely comprehending asked, "What kind of danger?"

"Something dreadful is going on up there."

"You have probably had a bad dream."

"No. I have seen red in the sky above Twin Peaks in the blackness. It is not dawn nor is it sunset. It means only one thing, blood."

"We'll leave at first light," Great Bear assured her.

VII

Great Bear was the first to reach the scene of the murder closely followed by Standing Bear and six of his finest warriors. Though hardened to death, they stood stunned, shocked by the scene that met their eyes - the blood spattered rocks, the blood streaked body, the bloody hair with the two owl feathers. They turned the body over and as one gasped at the horror of the face - beaten beyond recognition.

Great Bear knelt, touched an arm already turned gray as if to assure himself that White Owl was truly dead. He tentatively traced a tear in the deerskin shirt, felt the laceration beneath it. He looked up at Standing Bear, his face set, burdened, only his eyes betraying the pain he felt. His mouth moved wordlessly. Then scarcely audible from his lips came the one word, "Grizzly."

Standing Bear nodded somberly in agreement.

Great Bear rose, walked up to the cairn, raised his two clenched fists skyward and in a tortured voice irreverently asked, "Why?" His arms dropped slowly to his sides and slowly he turned back.

"White Owl's knife is missing," Standing Bear offered. And then, "He must have buried it in the bear."

Great Bear nodded taking some solace from the assumption and then sadly, "We'll move him down beyond the rocks where the grass and flowers grow and cover him with stones as is our custom."

They laid him in a bed of yellow alpine flowers, and before they placed the stones over him Great Bear laid his own flint knife in White Owl's right hand, "To guard you on your way to the other world."

Then he touched White Owl lightly one last time.

As they pulled up to the beach at the camping grounds, they saw She Who Sees waiting alone at the edge of the forest. Darkness was gathering behind her. She stood out in the sky's afterglow tall, erect, serene, even though she recognized the dread of telling on Great Bear's tortured face. He walked resolutely up to her, took her hand in his. "White Owl - he's with the Guardian Spirits."

Her voice trembled, "Dead?"

"Yes."

"How did he die?"

"It appeared to be a grizzly attack. If it is any comfort, he died bravely. His knife was missing, undoubtedly embedded in the beast's body."

"The plotting of the wicked Amte'p he who would harm us," She Who Sees said softly.

Great Bear saw the grieving in her eyes and took her in his arms, pressed her cheek to his and felt the wetness of her tears. She whispered, "They are watching at the canoes. They mustn't see our weakness," and she pushed away and walked back to their lodge. He followed her and once inside again took her into his arms. She heard him start to speak, "I'm sorry" - heard the words catch - "I was wrong. I..." She placed a finger to his lips..."You were not wrong. He had to go alone. Better this way than let fear rule his life."

There were three days of mourning. White Eagle returned late in the afternoon of the first day. He was devastated when told. They thought as one, talked as one, the same words often coming out of their mouths at the same time.

Perhaps the hardest part of all would be for She Who Sees to see White Eagle often deep in thought, the loneliness in him, his disinterest in the things he normally so enjoyed. He had gone on quest a boy and returned a man, but even for a man his grief was a terrible burden to bare. It would get better for all of them, time does that.

Later she spoke to grandmother and grandmother suggested, "Why don't you go huckleberrying?"

"Oh, grandmother that's a wonderful idea. I'll suggest it to Great Bear."

When she told Great Bear what grandmother had suggested, he hastened to agree. "The three of us. It's been long since we've done anything together. Standing Bear can take over while we're gone."

And in rising enthusiasm, "We'll take two canoes. One for you and me. One for White Eagle."

"Food and sleeping furs in ours," She Who Sees put in, smiling, the first time in days. "Bark baskets to bring back dried berries in White Eagle's canoe."

They left early the next morning before the camp started to stir for it would be a long day of paddling to the upper lake. As they turned the point and the encampment fell from view, She Who Sees spirits rose and it seemed as though this idyl would never end. She felt free, the past only a dream that never was. Only once as they neared No Quosh Kol Island and her eyes wandered over to Twin Peaks did the pain briefly rise and then was gone as the bulk of the island blotted out the view of the peaks and crypt there.

Soon they passed the sandy point that reached out from the northern corner of the island and into the channel when White Eagle challenged, "Race you to Pictured Rocks!"

Great Bear dug deep with his paddle into its waters, and their canoe leapt ahead. They raced neck and neck. Then as they reached Pictured Rocks, She Who Sees picked up a paddle. She giggled like a little girl as she and Great Bear pulled ahead of White Eagle. They reached Pictured Rocks first. They all doubled up with laughter. Great Bear felt as though a great weight had lifted from his shoulders. She Who Sees felt young again - and White Eagle felt as one with his parents.

They rounded the rocks and out onto the broad waters of Lake Chal Qe Lee. It was still early morning, cool, the waters flat, mists rising. It was as if they had come into a mystic new world and time.

The haunting call of a loon came across the water. As a little girl She Who Sees had thought the loons were spirits calling to her. When she grew older and came to know the stately creatures, their call stirred deep emotions within her and she loved to hear them speaking.

They paddled steadily, up through the narrows, past Twin Islands, out onto another wide expanse of water. A ripple was forming warning of higher waves to come. From here they hugged the shoreline. White caps built up by the time they reached the head of the lake. It was hot, the sun high over head. A white sandy bar extended out into the lake here marking the mouth of the Thorofare, a winding waterway that connected the lower lake to the upper lake. High waves beat upon the bar, but when they rounded it and entered the Thorofare all was calm, quiet. Tall alpine fir and cedar that grew along its banks protected it from the wind.

Fish darted ahead of their canoes. Not far into the channel they came upon a broad antlered moose standing in a marshy area to their left. It lifted its head and watched unconcernedly as they paddled past.

The Thorofare was at the height of its beauty. Along its banks light green ferns and yellow flags, and lavender flowering bushes grew. They paddled slowly, quietly; passed ducks sunning on logs that extended out into the water, an osprey nest perched high on top a bare snag. Three fuzzy young ospreys peered over its edge. They saw the mother osprey flying ahead of them, saw it sweep down and rise with a fish clutched in its talons.

Finally they rounded a gentle bend, down a straightaway, and out onto the open waters of the upper lake. High mountain peaks rose abruptly from its shores, 'sd SHAH' Mountain on the left. By now it was late afternoon. The waters lay flat and as they paddled up lake, close to the base of 'sd SHAH' Mountain, trout dimpled the surface, swallows and night hawks swooped about feeding on the hatching insects.

Near the head of the lake they beached their canoes on a small point of land. A small stream, runoff from 'sd SHAH' Mountain, entered the lake here. It provided cold, clear drinking water. A high flat bench rose behind the beach and here they made camp.

Great Bear and White Eagle built two lean-to shelters with pole frames thatched with cedar branches. They placed a circle of stones in front of them. Then while She Who Sees made beds of furs and built a fire, Great Bear and White Eagle went fishing.

They dug a few grubs from a rotten log to bait their bone hooks. They paddled out to the drop-off, and fast as they cast a baited hook into the water a cutthroat trout hit it. They soon had enough for that night and morning the next day.

As they returned to camp, they heard a loud resonant booming sound as though from a giant drum. Startled, never having heard the sound, White Eagle turned to Great Bear, "What was that?"

"A beaver, a warning slap of its broad tail on the water when someone intrudes on its domain."

"I was afraid it might be the evil one Amte'p," White Eagle whispered.

Later around the campfire as they were eating the juicy crisp trout, roasted on spits over glowing coals, a doe followed by a broad antlered black tail deer passed by unhurriedly down to the water to drink. From time to time the deer turned their heads to inspect the watchers, wide eyed, unconcernedly. Then they ambled down the beach, stopping occasionally to snatch a blade of grass and faded off into the blackness.

For some time they were quiet, their thoughts resting on the visit of the deer, the beauty of the night, the blackness of the mountains, the mystery of the points of light in the sky, some brighter than the rest, some blinking.

"A most precious idyl, here with the two men I love most in all the world," She Who Sees mused.

They moved closer to the fire, as the coolness came down upon them from the mountain behind. She Who Sees pulled her knees up under her and rested her chin upon them. Beside her, Great Bear and White Eagle sat, their eyes fastened on the fire, their faces lighted by its glow.

"White Eagle, have I ever told you of the Legend of the Lake?" She Who Sees asked softly.

"No."

"Well, legend handed down to me by my Grandmother tells that the upper lake is shaped like a woman and no one shall ever drown in it. If you were to climb 'sd SHAH' Mountain, you would see that."

"Some day I will do that," White Owl said with interest rising.

"The lower lake is shaped like a man and people have drowned in it. Coyote, the mischief maker, can cause the wind to whip up violent storms to punish us. We must always be cautious when out on its waters."

"And punish us he does if ever we're careless," Great Bear put in. "I've been caught out in the middle when the waves have quickly risen and driven me to the shelter of a cove or island. Better to skirt the shore when possible."

They sat in the embracing comfort of the fire, watched contentedly 'til they started to nod, and then they turned to their warm fur beds.

A trail worn smooth by countless generations of berry pickers led off from the rear of camp and up 'sd SHAH' Mountain to the berry patches. Along the early parts of the trail where the forest was dense, the bushes were tall, spindly, and the berries were small. But as the trail rose up the sides of the mountain the forest opened up, and there were berry bushes everywhere as far as they could see loaded with berries.

She Who Sees laughed delightedly, "Look at these berries, they're so big this year." She loved to pick huckleberries.

"Big as your thumbnail," Great Bear put in. He hadn't picked berries since his youth on Chsawl cestkum. It brought back a wave of nostalgic memories. Being a chief it wasn't proper to pick berries, but here with She Who Sees and White Eagle, with no witnesses, he savored the moment.

In the meantime, White Eagle had wandered off looking for bigger, better berries. The biggest berries and the bushes with the most berries usually grew in the shade of trees and in hollows. When he found a good patch he'd call to She Who Sees and Great Bear and they'd come over to pick.

They picked the largest, the blue black ones. She Who Sees would sit on a log or on the ground, pull a bush over her with one hand and strip the berries off into a small 'koxa-e' pe', bark basket, with the other.

When it was full, she'd dump it into a 'SCHEE le 'kwa', larger bark pannier. She was the nimblest, the fastest picker.

By noon the heat rose, and they stopped at an icy rivulet to quench their thirst. Large cedars grew along its banks. They sat by one, leaned up against its smooth, warm bark. She Who Sees produced a few camas cakes and strips of dried venison for them to munch on.

Once during the afternoon they heard a crackling of bushes and came upon a large black bear and her two yearling cubs raking berries off the bushes. She smelled them but couldn't see them being nearsighted and shooed the cubs up a tree.

"We'll leave this patch to them." Great Bear whispered, and they backed off and detoured around.

They picked through the heat of the day perspiring profusely. Then vagrant mountain breezes came in the late afternoon, played about them, keeping them cool. From time to time they drank from pools of the tiny streams that sprang from the hillsides, so cold it made their teeth throb. By mid-afternoon they had all the berries they could carry in the backpack panniers. They cached the small picking baskets by the side of the trail and set off back to camp.

They were nearing camp when a brood of fool hens hopped out of the path ahead and onto low hanging branches. They walked up to them, and when White Eagle picked up a heavy stick and touched one it merely moved further back on the limb. Unlike its cousin the ruffed grouse, which would have flown off, it eyed White Eagle interestedly, bobbed and twisted its head about. The others, their backs turned, ignored White Eagle, their interest being directed elsewhere. He brought six down with a sharp rap to the head. He turned to Great Bear, smiling satisfied, "They give themselves to us so easily. A wonder any are left."

"Perhaps because you don't see them often," Great Bear offered. "And they have large broods."

That night, hot off the spits and next day cold when they stopped berry picking for lunch, they had the fool hens. Not as tasty nor tender as ruffed grouse, but out in the open when you've been working, a treat.

The next day and the next they picked huckleberries, and then having enough to fill the storage compartments under the bow and stern of the canoes, Great Bear and White Eagle took off to scout the caribou herds in the mountains across the lake. There were numerous game trails leading back to the high peaks. In the small valleys and mountain cirques they found bands of caribou. Along the rocky crest they saw numerous white specs, moving specs, mountain goats the finest of all game meat. It was an area seldom visited and the game unaccustomed to humans, unafraid. "They'll be easily hunted, Great Bear said, "And there are many. More than I have ever seen this time of year. We'll return with a hunting party in the fall."

She Who Sees had thought she was getting over her loss, but when Great Bear and White Eagle left the pain welled up. It was the first time she had been alone since the tragedy and seeing one broad backed son going off alone with Great Bear, when always there had been two, the two of them so close, almost like one, it tore at her like no other loss ever had.

She must get busy. Get her mind off herself, try not to think of what might have been. "I will dry the berries, at least partially. It will preserve them from spoiling and lighten the load on the trip back," she thought.

She laid tanned deerskin pelts on the ground and covered them with berries. From time to time she rolled the berries over exposing a different surface to the hot sun.

Though she concentrated on the task, occasionally a vision of White Owl would break through her determination. She could not accept that he was truly gone. If only she had seen with her own eyes his lifeless body, perhaps to touch, to caress one last time. But without seeing, there was no finality. Perhaps Great Bear would take her there some day.

VIII

White Owl's reaction to being wrenched out of sleep and bound had been one of anger, anger that turned to horror when with no emotion, Black Hawk brutally murdered his own man. He feared he too would be killed. But then it occurred to him, if his hands were tied behind his back, he was not to be killed, at least not yet. Then the thought occurred, a worse fate, perhaps he was to become a slave of some distant tribe; no hope of rescue, because he would be considered dead.

The cunning Black Hawk did not take the trade route, but rather the rocky, trackless crest of the mountains, as a precaution, in case the ruse of White Owl's death were recognized. The terrain along the east slope was rough, rugged, strewn with granite boulders. With his hands tied behind his back and a noose added around his neck, White Owl moved slowly and no amount of jerking from the warrior at the other end of his leash would speed him up.

They fell behind. Black Hawk stormed back. "Move faster. We've got to be off this bald slope by daybreak or we can be seen!"

"It's no good. He keeps falling. Loses his balance." the guard replied.

Black Hawk studied the situation a moment and then untied White Owl's hands, looped a thong over his head put another man at the other end behind him. With a warrior fore and aft, they could control him completely, yet keep up.

By daybreak they had moved off the barren rocky crest into sparsely forested alpine country. Black Hawk kept a steady pace stopping only for water at streams they crossed. As time passed, White Owl sensed that his captors held him in awe, even fear. When he would leap over a downed log or across a rivulet, and grasp his medicine bag to keep it from swinging about, he would see their brows knit and concern, even fear, rise in their eyes. "Perhaps," he thought, "they fear my medicine and if so I can use that against them."

They moved easily, swiftly through this new terrain. By nightfall they reached a bluff high above the ntxwe river. In a small alpine basin, they made camp and built a fire. It was out of sight with water nearby. They each had a small ration of dried buffalo. "Buffalo meat! These people are from the east, buffalo hunters," he surmised.

Afterwards when they sat by the fire, Black Hawk and his men huddled together talking in low voices. White Owl caught a word now and then. He absentmindedly picked up a smooth rounded pebble, and rolled it around in his hand. Then he flipped the pebble into the air, caught it, opened his hand and it was empty, reached under his armpit and pulled out the stone.

Their voices stopped. Their eyes rolled in fear as the stone rolled about in his hand. Magic was a part of a Shaman's medicine. She Who Sees had taught him of it, but among the No Quosh Kol it was used only to transfer the sick persons mind from himself to faith in the cure.

Black Hawk regained his composure and quickly re-tied White Owl's feet together and his hands behind his back before he could wave his hand and do more serious mischief - perhaps make their weapons disappear. He placed a guard over him for the night.

The next morning, while it was still dark, they left the basin and descended the ridge top to the valley of the ntxwe. Along its banks lay a trade route to the east. This was land familiar to White Owl. He had traveled by canoe up the ntxwe many times to visit the Upper No Quosh Kol. Their village was located where the ntxwe river flowed out of lake ntxwe.

Black Hawk turned up stream, the others following closely in single file. The trail was broad, worn smooth by centuries of foot traffic. It followed the twists and turns of the mighty ntxwe, which in No Quosh Kol tongue symbolically reduces all other streams to lesser status. At first light they left the trail and holed up in dense cover along the banks of a feeder stream out of sight of anyone passing on the trade route.

The morning passed slowly, gradually warming, and with the heat came the large biting fly. A muffled oath and a slap broke the silence. Black Hawk raised his atlatl to silence the offender, thought better of it, and moved them to higher ground where breezes kept the insects away. At noon, they had a ration of dried buffalo. Throughout the afternoon they dozed.

In the evening, they returned to the trade route. Before long they neared the village of the upper No Quosh Kol. Here the trade route turned north, up and around the vast expanse of lake ntxwe. The sound of barking dogs rose from the village. They left the trail upon hearing the dogs and made a wide detour around the village.

They moved at a steady pace around the north end of the lake and down the east side. At dawn they came upon the upper ntxwe river flowing in from the east. Here the trade route turned up-river. They made camp on a low bench from which they could observe the route, yet not be seen themselves.

The night had been uneventful, they had met no one, but two nights later they came upon a single man by a campfire. He was a courier and couriers carried tales. Black Hawk walked up to him smiling and without warning seized the man and drove his long flint knife deep under his rib cage. The man fell to his knees, and then pitched over on his face, his life blood running on the ground.

"He won't carry any more tales," Black Hawk said matter-of-factly. And then, "Take his pack, we'll divide it later."

White Owl restrained himself from showing any emotion. They would consider it weakness. It was a heinous act, cruelty beyond understanding, the Flathead a gentle man, completely trusting. But there was nothing he could do. Two of the warriors picked the body up and carried it off into the woods.

The next night they reached the great bend of the ntxwe. It was growing light when they came to a sizeable stream that entered the ntxwe from a deep cut in the mountains on the other side. Here the ntxwe ran smoothly. It was shallow. They plunged into the waters and splashed across. A well worn path led up the right side of the stream and Black Hawk strode boldly onto it as one who considered it his own.

This day they did not lay up and rest. By mid-morning they came to a fork in the stream. Black Hawk took the left fork that tumbled out of a narrow ravine. The trail rose rapidly, and before long they broke out onto a grass covered valley walled in by granite escarpments. Beyond rose the crest of the Bitterroots. At the far end of the valley nestled a village of white tepees. A sentinel waved them on.

"A veritable fortress," White Owl thought. "Escape would be nearly impossible."

White Owl's eyes wandered over the valley as they walked towards the village. Through it ran the stream, its course marked by a line of willows. It disappeared into a cleft in the valley wall beyond the village - an escape route if not guarded. As they approached the village they were met by clamoring dogs.

It was readily apparent to White Owl as they entered that these were not happy people as in the No Quosh Kol villages. There the children bounded about animatedly at games. The young women tended the cooking fires, the drying racks, prepared foods; always smiling, chattering happily among themselves. The grandmothers sat contentedly by the lodge's openings sewing, and supervising the children. The men gathered in clutches busily engaged in making flint tools, flint points, repairing their canoes.

Here they were somber. The children and young mothers and grandmothers were listless. They did not chatter happily among themselves. They seemed subdued. He saw many slaves, emaciated, ill clad creatures, tending the cookfires, the drying racks, carrying water.

The men were warriors, fully armed, their faces blackened. They were shorter than the No Quosh Kol, well muscled fighting men. He was to learn that the Ravens were raiders and lived by the spoils of their raids. They struck quickly under the cover of night. Anyone following them was quickly dispatched in the narrow confines of the entrance.

Black Hawk led the way to a wide, circular area in the middle of the village. In its center was a large fire pit encircled with fire blackened stones. The ground around was beaten smooth, a sign of victory dances following successful raids.

One tepee, larger than all the rest, stood out from the others, and over its opening were hung two jet black raven wings. The sides were rolled up knee high to let the summer breezes and light enter. Under the edge, White Owl could see the lower portions of several seated figures. Evidently the sentinel had signaled their arrival and the council of Ravens had been assembled. The nooses were removed from around his neck, and Black Hawk signaled for him to follow. White Owl noticed a change come over Black Hawk. Sweat broke out revealing the apprehension he was struggling to conceal.

They stepped through the opening and Black Hawk stopped before the central figure a powerfully built man. He wore three black feathers in his hair symbol of a chieftain, Chief Thunder Raven. Black Hawk bowed slightly and in a low subservient voice announced, "I have brought you White Owl."

Chief Thunder Raven asked grimly, "Were you followed?"

And Black Hawk said, "We were not followed and we never will be." And then he told of the ruse and how they left no tracks.

Thunder Raven leaned back and nodded in satisfied approval, "You have done well. Leave White Owl with us."

He sat impassively for several moments after Black Hawk left. He stared thoughtfully into White Owl's eyes. White Owl stared back boldly. He stood calmly, his bearing and manner that of a son of a chieftain.

"Remove the thongs from his wrists," Thunder Raven ordered, and when that was done he picked up a long stemmed catlinite pipe that had rested at his feet. He lit it ceremoniously, drew a deep puff, exhaled it slowly towards the opening in the apex of the tepee, and then passed it among the council. Then he passed it to White Owl.

Though he felt a great revulsion for Thunder Raven and his council, he took the pipe in his hand and putting it to his lips, took a deep draft and blew the smoke up towards the aperture in the ceiling as he had seen those before him do.

Thunder Raven motioned for him to take a seat. "Once we were a people of the plains," his voice was deep, somber. "Our land was wide and the buffalo many. There was always food. Our children were fat, our women slim and beautiful, our warriors strong, fearless. Our enemies respected us for we were the Ravens the strongest, the most feared nation on all the plains."

"Then one winter many generations ago a pestilence descended upon us. Many died and those that were left were weakened."

"Word of our misfortune spread and early one summer morning our enemies descended upon us and drove us off our bountiful lands. We fled over the mountains."

"The Blackfoot, the Flathead fell upon us killing more of our people, driving us into these mountains. Here we are safe. A handful of our warriors have withstood many in the narrow ravine below. Bones of many enemy remain."

"You bring great power to the Ravens. One day we shall regain our lands." And then speaking as one who is about to bestow a great gift, "You shall be a Raven. Have your choice of our most beautiful maidens. I have no son. You shall be my son. You shall have a tepee of your own to sleep in. During the days you shall be at my side."

White Owl was astonished. The blind arrogance of the tyrant, to think that he would give up his own people, his homeland. But he inclined his head slightly as if to acknowledge Thunder Raven's beneficence. To do otherwise, he knew, would be fatal. But in reality he was thinking of the possible escape route and planning to explore it at the earliest opportunity.

IX

The tamarack were turning a soft orange and the quaking aspen an iridescent yellow. The snows that had dusted the mountain tops across Lake Chal Qe Lee, each day edged further down the mountain sides. The skies were bluer, the sun brighter, almost blinding at certain angles. Throbbing colored lights filled the nighttime skies to the north. The days were cooler. Lake Chal Qe Lee lay flat, gray, the morning mists that rose from it burned off by noon. Vast flights of ducks and geese flew over daily.

It was a time She Who Sees loved, 'stitch AY,' the lull between summer and winter. The ache in her heart was lessening. The loss of White Owl had been the greatest burden she ever had to bear. The canoe trip with Great Bear and White Eagle to the upper lake, being truly alone with them had been a healing.

They had returned with the canoes loaded low with huckleberries. Huckleberrying had been good throughout the Kaniksu, and a large supply of dried berries had been backpacked across the mountains to the village on the ntxwe. The early summer runs of cutthroat had been bountiful and the fall runs of whitefish had filled the streams from bank to bank. The supplies of fish sent over the mountains were the largest She Who Sees could remember.

Hunting parties had returned from across the lake with many mountain goat and bear and black tailed deer. Their hides would make many moccasins and clothing, the horns and antlers tools.

Great Bear and White Eagle had returned to the upper lake with a party of hunters to hunt the caribou. This time they had camped at the sandy beach on the north side of the lake near the mouth of the stream that drained the vast range of the caribou. Whitefish were still running up the stream, and each morning they feasted on fresh caught fish. Many caribou and mountain goat had fallen prey to their powerful atlatls.

In the beginning, it had seemed the summer idyl at Lake Chal Qe Lee would never end. There had been the first walk down to the beach to let her eyes sweep across the blue waters past Papoose Island, on along the mountain crest from Notch Mountain to Sentinel Mountain to the north, the quick glance to see if the osprey still nested on the old snag at the point. Then at the midway point there came the sad realization that the summer was slipping by and now the sweet torture of daily countdown to an ending. Yet she was young and could tell herself there would be other summers to come.

A day hardly passed now that some family did not pack and return to the winter village on the ntxwe. Winters there were milder than at Lake

Chal Qe Lee, less snow. The great supplies of meat had been transported over the mountains and the drying racks were now stored in the shelter of the trees back from the beach.

Then one morning there was a skiff of snow on the ground and Great Bear said it was time to leave. Even the lower passes in the mountains would soon be filling with snow. The last of the canoes were moved to pole racks and placed bottoms down. The lodge mats were stored underneath them. She Who Sees and White Eagle walked down to the beach for a final look at the lake and the mountains beyond.

X

It had been hard leaving Lake Chal Qe Lee, but She Who Sees soon became caught up in the routine of daily life in the village and the summer became just another dream to run through her mind on bleak winter nights. It was good to be back in her warm, comfortable winter home. Theirs was the largest in the village with separate cooking and sleeping wing and a great room where village celebrations were held and Great Bear met with his council of elders.

Here along the ntxwe river was the traditional homeland of the No Quosh Kol. It was vast, stretching hundreds of miles up and down the ntxwe including the land and lakes and mountains and smaller tributary rivers on either side.

The river itself was a highway along which the No Quosh Kol moved daily in their sturgeon nosed canoes. It gave them great freedom of movement. It gave them access to the vast camas beds along its flood plains. With an assured food supply, there was leisure time available for cultural development and social relationships.

Not long after they returned from Lake Chal Qe Lee, snow came to the valley. The rust colored long lodges of the village turned white, the laughter of children was stilled. The only movements were the curling wisps of grey smoke of cooking fires, like breath, rising out of smoke holes on the roof tops.

Winter in the village was a time when the men repaired and replaced their tools and hunting atlatls and points and gear and the women made new deerskin moccasins and apparel and repaired the old. They decorated them with root dies and quills. It was a time for socializing. The lodges were warm, secure. Two or three families lived in a single lodge fifty or more feet long and twelve feet wide. The lodges had a frame work constructed of peeled poles over which 'ts TSAUtl ke,' tule mats, were laid. Dirt was heaped up against the walls in winter to keep the heat in. Older people lived closer to the end opening and younger people at the center of the lodge.

The women cooked the meals over central fires sharing them with families across the central strip. They kept their food in the storage area nearest their own sleeping and working areas. The great quantity of food obtained in the summer and fall was stored on raised racks outside. Food was the property of the tribe as a whole and was distributed under the direction of Great Bear.

The food was stored high enough to be safe from rodents. However from time to time food was found to be missing and was accompanied by the heavy, musky smell of yeti or Sasquatch. Some of the elders claimed to have seen them and reported them to be hairy upright creatures that walked like man only they were much taller. They were shy and quickly disappeared.

There was leisure time for games. The most popular adult game was the stick game often accompanied with gambling. There was also a dice like game played with beaver teeth. The children spun bark tops but were expected to play quietly - no running around or shouting. In good weather they played outside. At mid winter a medicine dance was held. Evenings were a time for storytelling.

Winter was a busy time for She Who Sees. There were the evil plots of Amte'p and hostile shamans that were to be thwarted through her spirit powers and skill. There were more illnesses to be treated at this time of year with medicines and incantations passed down by shamans before her. She was the most skillful and considered to have the greatest powers of all the No Quosh Kol shamans up and down the ntxwe. There were smaller villages, offshoots of the main village, with their own sub-chiefs to whom she was called to treat the sick and injured.

It was shortly after the winter Medicine Dance that the vision came to She Who Sees one night. She had been asleep for some time when she felt bathed in an aura of love and brightness. Then out of the brightness came a vision of White Owl. He was smiling lovingly, and words came though his lips did not move...come home." The vision faded slowly and she wakened.

The aura of love remained and she felt a great happiness. But it was all so strange. Was White Owl reaching out to her from the spirit world, and what meaning did the words have? They were incomplete. Was it just a dream or was it a vision or merely the madness of a long winter night?

And then not long after, she began having dreams in which she was searching for White Owl. There was a pattern to the dreams, a desperate looking through a village, peopled with strange people, spectral people, none talking to her, the feeling that she'd been there before, light that blurred the sudden appearance of White Owl, and her plea "Come back with me." And then he was someone else and would fade away, and she'd realize that he was dead. She'd awaken and wonder why the dreams kept recurring. Were the Guardian Spirits speaking to her? Was there a message here?

She wanted to wake Great Bear and tell him of her dreams but couldn't bear to take him from a sound sleep. He had other problems weighing on his mind. In the bright light of morning, it all seemed rather foolish and she never mentioned it to him.

Great Bear was now grooming White Eagle to one day become chief of all the No Quosh Kols. White Eagle sat at his right at all council meetings and religious ceremonies. He accompanied him on visits to sub-chiefs in smaller No Quosh Kol villages up and down the ntxwe. White Eagle was now as tall as Great Bear. He had the bearing of a leader and his words were gaining respect and attention at council meetings.

His days were filled, but in the evenings his thoughts sometimes turned to White Owl. The brutal scene at Twin Peaks would flash across his mind and the ache of losing would return. There was something about it that raised vague stirrings, but he could never place a finger on it.

About the time the snows were deepest, the days getting noticeably longer, and the diet of dried camas, dried berries and meat monotonous, everyone in the village with the exception of the elderly and women in the advanced stages of pregnancy took off on a winter hunt. The deep snows had forced the deer by this time to migrate to lower elevations where they gathered in herds in valleys rich in browse.

The winter hunt was a highlight of the season, a celebration, a release of spirits pent up by long confinement in crowded lodges. An air of excitement spread through the village when Great Bear had announced the hunt.

That night there was dancing of the "sinkakua," the hunting dance, in the great hall. Flames from the great fire pit in the center of the hall leapt high reflecting off the swaying, twisting, glistening bodies of the dancers and cast their gyrating shadows on the mat walls. Drummers beat out hypnotic rhythms on stiff rawhide circles placed on the dry bare ground. Dancers sang their sacred medicine songs and songs of successful hunts. Between the songs they boasted of hunting exploits. Women onlookers also sang their medicine songs and as the beat picked up swayed to the haunting drumbeat.

Great Bear finally raised his hand and signed for the drummers to stop and motioned for a male shaman to step forward. His body was painted with hunting symbols. He sang the ritualistic hunting song, performed leaping dances, shook rattles, offered up prayers and incantations to the Guardian Spirits for successful hunting.

The next morning, early, the families filled backpack baskets with food, extra clothing, sleeping furs and rolled tule mats. The hunters took an extra supply of darts for their atlatls and tied talismans in their hair to assure successful hunting and to protect themselves.

Excitement filled the air as they took off on the Sylvus trail. The children, released from the confines of the lodges, chattered happily, and parents had to caution them to be quiet lest they stampede the game to higher ground. They wore snowshoes, the men going first packing the snow down for the children and women to follow.

The hunt shaman led the way. From time to time he stopped and waved a wand festooned with tail and tine of deer in the four directions to ward off misfortunes and machinations that might be spawned by hostile shamans and evil spirits. He made a show of checking various sites for their hunting camp finally choosing a mountain meadow with ample space for several lodges, spring water and a supply of dead down timber for fires.

The women created temporary lodges, a framework of poles over which they spread balsam fir branches and tule mats. Meanwhile White Eagle and several scouts went out to check the surrounding area for game. They returned at dusk, and reported having seen small herds scattered throughout the area in sheltered hollows and cedar swamps.

They had come across six deer in a deep pocket of snow. The deer attempted to flee, and they had overtaken them on their snowshoes. They dispatched them with clubs, gutted them out on the spot and dragged the carcases to camp.

Pairs of women fell to butchering the carcases. First they carefully removed the hides. Then they scraped the hides clean of all scraps of flesh with their sharp flint scrapers.

Next they stripped the meat from the bones, set them aside to be cracked later and the marrow removed. The meat was then apportioned equally to all families by Great Bear.

The aroma of fresh venison soon arose throughout the camp from chunks of meat propped on sticks over cooking fires. It was a feast, a celebration of the first fresh meat of the season. Prayers were offered. The men ritually took the first bites and then all gorged themselves.

Snowflakes were falling gently when the hunters set out early the next morning. They followed the tracks of the day before, still showing through the dusting of snow. Soon they came upon the scene of the kill of yesterday. Several ravens that were arguing over scraps overlooked by scavengers of the night took flight.

Beyond rose a sharp ridge, a torturous climb in the deep soft snow and occasional down timber. White Eagle reached the top first.

Here on the ridge top it was open tall pine. Below lay a wide valley with a sizeable stream flowing through it. It was there, yesterday, that they had found a herd of deer yarded up in a thick growth of cedar that grew along the stream.

"What we'll do," White Eagle said when the others had caught up with him, "Is put a line of hunters across the valley below the cedars. They'll be the blockers. That's the way the deer are going to go, downstream. We'll put a few hunters at the upper end to drive the deer out of the yard."

To the young hunter who asked "What if they go out the sides?" he said patiently, being the boy must learn, "A deer or two may go out the sides, but the herd instinct will carry most the easy way out...downstream. We'll pick up the stragglers that go out the side later in the deep snows."

White Eagle watched as the two groups fanned out and stole down the hillside bent low as possible on their snowshoes, like ghosts flitting from cover to cover, the falling snow blurring their movements. Ah, the excitement of it, the tension building as they neared their positions. Would a sentinel buck spot them and the whole herd bolt downstream before they reached their positions?

"White Owl, if only he were here to share this with me," he mused. "But drive it from your mind. The if onlys are the artful deceit of Amte'p designed to seduce, and weaken my resolve."

Back to the hunt, concentrate on the now. They were nearing their positions, and it was up to him to set things in motion. The blockers reached their positions first, hunkering down behind bush or fallen tree, so as not to be seen. The lead beater waved ready. White Eagle pursed his lips and blew a shrill blast, said to waken the spirits. The beaters, those who had the circles of stiff rawhide, beat on them and the others pounded sticks and clubs on tree trunks. They shouted and waved their arms wildly.

It wasn't long before the first deer attempted to slip out the lower end. The blockers let them slip by, then took them with their atlatls before they got too far out.

The beaters moved further into the cedars and the herd moved as one out of the yard. It became a wild melee of leaping, swerving, darting animals, blockers leaping to their feet, loosing their darts at the passing deer. It was now too dangerous to shoot in the direction of the advancing beaters despite the dense forest between.

From where White Eagle stood, it looked like a battlefield. Many of the deer were evading the blockers and disappearing downstream. But even more were falling to the powerful atlatls. The hunters were so skilled they could down objects thrown into the air in practice. One mad wild rush and then it was over. It lasted but a few minutes, leaving black shapes and widening red circles against the white snow.

White Eagle plunged down the hillside to the line of hunters now standing silently among their kill. They stood with heads bowed in prayer, thanking the deer for giving themselves to them.

White Eagle offered up thanks to the deer and then to the Guardian Spirits for the bounty of their gift. There was always the regret for him, viewing the lifeless form of a creature that only moments before had been so lovely, remembering other times he had happened on one in some small meadow feeding, the deer throwing its head up in alarm, looking at him with its large round trusting eyes, pawing the ground before it questioningly, and then, deciding he meant no harm this time, continued feeding. Seeing them always pleased him.

Again that night there was the feasting and celebrating, the dancing, the singing, the boasting of the hunters, the pantomimes of the events of the hunt, the onlookers hanging on their every word, their every gesture.

Early the next morning, not long before light, She Who Sees was awakened by Owl calling to her. She went to the opening of the lodge and saw Owl in a tree nearby, silhouetted against the sky, "What is it Owl?"

"One has died."

"Who?" She Who Sees asked her, voice choked, fearful.

"Grandmother, mother of Great Bear," Owl intoned.

"Oh no," She Who Sees murmured. "Not now, not so soon after White Owl." She turned and slowly returned to the sleeping furs, dreading telling Great Bear and White Eagle. She stood several minutes looking down on them. She shook Great Bear and then White Eagle. They rose on their elbows, questioning looks on their faces.

"Owl..." she hesitated, "has just brought a message to me. It is grandmother."

"Is she..." and Great Bear couldn't finish it.

"Yes, she is dead," She Who Sees answered softly, compassionately.

"I did not expect it this soon," Great Bear replied, his voice quieted by sorrow.

"It seemed she'd be here always," White Eagle looked questioningly from one to the other.

Men are never prepared, She Who Sees thought, they expect things will always be the same. She had seen it coming, seen the little changes, the tiredness, the longer sleep, the slowing walk, the indecision. She did not speak of it. It would only have lengthened the sadness.

"Go tell Standing Bear to break camp and return to the village, White Eagle," Great Bear said somberly. "We will leave as soon as you return."

They placed grandmother on a high bench overlooking the ntxwe river with extra moccasins and a doeskin bag of dried camas bulbs for the long journey to the spirit land. She rested on a tule mat and her body was covered with furs to keep her warm and over the furs, heaped high, were washed river stones of many colors.

XI

It was not long after his capture that White Owl first attempted to escape. He had been treated well enough, given a tepee to himself at the far edge of the village where the stream flowed out of a cleft in the valley wall. It nestled in a peaceful glade of aspen. "Quiet except for the quaking of leaves, where you can meditate and commune with the spirits," Thunder Raven had offered in a kindly tone, entirely out of character. His brutal side he reserved for all others. He favored White Owl and it was resented by warrior sub-chiefs and council members yet none dared voice it. He had a guard placed at the entrance to White Owl's tepee - usually Black Hawk.

Often of an evening Thunder Raven would come to White Owl's tepee. They would talk and Thunder Raven would recount his exploits, an attempt to impress White Owl. Black Hawk had told him of White Owl's mystic power of making things disappear, and he never tired of seeing the feat performed. His eyes would pop as the object moved from the present to the spirit world and then back.

One night when Thunder Raven came by, White Owl was practicing passing the Stick Game Master stick back and forth in his hands. The Master stick was about the length of the middle finger and had a black band painted around its middle. He had the reflexes and movements of the magician. He could create the illusion of the stick moving back and forth from hand to hand, but all the time remaining in just the one. He was a champion among the No Quosh Kol.

Thunder Raven was fascinated. "Have you ever played Sticks," White Owl asked innocently.

"No."

"Sit down and I'll show you how," White Owl offered. "Now take the Master stick. Pass it back and forth. Get the feel of it."

"That's good. Now put it out of sight between your knees. Shuffle the stick back and forth. Bring your hands in front of you. No, don't look at your right hand. That's the one you have the stick in. Yes?"

"Yes!" Thunder Raven admitted.

"Always look directly into my eyes. Try to keep my eyes focused on your eyes, not your hands."

"It's a game of skill, outwitting, outguessing your opponent. Would you care to play a game?"

"Yes."

"Alright. Here are five sticks for you, a playing set, that is."

"Now I'll pass the Master back and forth, and you guess which hand it's in."

Thunder Raven pointed to the right hand. White Owl opened it and it was empty. "You lost that hand and I take one of your sticks. First one to take all of the sticks wins. Try again."

This time White Owl made it obvious that the stick went into his left hand and Thunder Raven pointed to that hand. "Good. Now you take the Master and I guess which hand you have it in."

White Owl let Thunder Raven win the game and then another. Then White Owl said, "You learn quickly. Next time we'll play for small stakes. Adds to the excitement."

"The sticks?" Thunder Raven asked, desire showing in the way he held them close.

"Keep them. I have others." White Owl replied immediately.

It was a few nights later when the village was quiet and Black Hawk had fallen asleep. White Owl slipped out of his tepee and entered the cleft in the wall. Ahead the canyon floor rose steeply, seemingly to disappear in the sky high above. Down this steep incline plunged the stream in a series of noisy falls and boisterous runs. Along its course a dim trail led upwards. White Owl took to the trail with some trepidation not knowing what might lie ahead.

In the dark canyon, he moved slowly placing his feet carefully to avoid stumbling over roots and stones in the trail. And then as his eyes adjusted to the darkness, he moved swiftly upwards. Soon he was climbing nearly straight up, reaching hand over hand, clutching at spindly bushes and scrub tree limbs to check his balance and pull himself up.

Once a vine pulled loose and he slid backwards. He was about to throw it away when he realized it was one of medicinal value and clutched it in his left hand. Nearing the top, the stream that had been growing smaller and smaller, suddenly disappeared among some large boulders. At last he reached what appeared to be, in the blackness of the night, a flat alpine meadow deep in coarse grass and edged with stout heavily limbed pines. The trail wound ahead towards the sharp black peaks of the Bitterroots.

He had moved but a short distance when a noose dropped over his shoulders, and he was thrown roughly to the ground. He looked up into the black painted face of a Raven warrior he had once seen in the village. His moccasined foot now pressed down on his neck shutting off his windpipe.

"What are you doing up here at this time of night?"

"Gathering medicines," and he frantically waved the vine in his face. "It's most powerful when gathered in the blackness of an overcast night." The Raven eyed him suspiciously..."I'll have to take you back to Black Hawk and see what he says," and hauling White Owl to his feet shoved him back down the trail.

At his tepee, White Owl had to repeat for Black Hawk, who wakened as they approached, that he was gathering medicinal vines whose leaves were most powerful in the blackness of an overcast night. Black Hawk reached for his bulging medicine bag, "You lie. You have food in there and were trying to escape."

White Owl drew back, pushed Black Hawk's hand aside. "I'd advise you not to touch it. Within is dust of spider and fang of rattlesnake. Powerful medicine, deadly if not handled properly." And then he drew his hand away daring Black Hawk to reach inside.

Black Hawk frowned, his eyes wavered, his hand trembled and he withdrew his hand. Then realizing he dare not take White Owl to Thunder Raven for punishment and reveal at the same time his dereliction of duty said, "I'll not report this to Thunder Raven, but I'm warning you—sneak out alone again and you'll have a fatal accident."

XII

Winter came early to the Bitterroots and the land of the Ravens and with it a change in their fortunes. Of late their raiding parties had suffered greater casualties, often returning empty handed. Their enemies had posted more sentinels further out from their villages. Now, warned of Raven movements, they intercepted them.

But the Raven raiders changed tactics sweeping down on their enemies out of snowstorms in the middle of the night. They moved like ghosts striking terror in the minds of the enemy. For they left no trace of humans having been there - no trace in the snow where they came from. To the enemy it seemed they must be spirit raiders and they were being punished by evil spirits.

They seized the enemy food supplies, carrying off what they could, destroying the remainder, leaving them weakened. As their enemies grew weaker and weaker, the Ravens grew stronger, emboldened. They thought that White Owl had brought great power to the Ravens and that they were invincible.

By spring they turned to killing men, women, and children - and taking the most beautiful women for slaves. They had become a scourge on the land.

White Owl was now being treated almost as a god. It troubled him deeply that he was the source of their power.

It was at this time that Thunder Raven brought a beautiful girl to White Owl. "For your pleasure, your reward," he said, a lewd grin spreading across his face. "She will be your slave—cook, sew, do your bidding. If she doesn't, beat her."

And with that Thunder Raven strode off. White Owl watched until he disappeared into the center of the village and then turned to look more carefully at the girl. She was slender, nearly as tall as he. Her hair was pulled back and tied at the nape with a blue lupine. He thought of She Who Sees and the resemblance was striking.

He found himself staring at her, caught in the soft warmth of her dark brown eyes. She looked up at him questioningly, shyly. He wanted to tell her she had nothing to fear from him, but Black Hawk was lingering nearby, his back turned to them but near enough to hear any word that was said and sure to report it to Thunder Raven.

He said brusquely, "Fetch a bark basket from the tepee, one sealed tight with pitch. I'll show you where to get drinking water. It'll be one of your duties to keep it filled."

There was a grace, a regalness to her movements and the thought crossed his mind that she must be of the upper class of her tribe. He led her to a quiet pool upstream, away from the regular village watering hole, a place he often turned to, to escape the noise and strife of the village— beyond earshot of Black Hawk. She filled the basket and turned to leave, but he placed a restraining hand on hers and in a low voice, "I am like you, a captive."

She rested her eyes questioningly on his. "You are not one of them?"

"I am a No Quosh Kol, White Owl, son of Great Bear, chief of the No Quosh Kols."

"Ah, we have heard of you and your brother, but you were..."

"...killed by a grizzly?" He smiled. "A ruse and I see it worked. And you?"

"I am of the Apakara. Ours was a small tribe, our numbers reduced by a rare disease. My father, who was chief of the Apakaras, my mother, my grandmother, my little sister all were murdered by the Ravens," her voice trailed off, a frown filled her forehead and anguish filled her eyes.

His hand tightened unconsciously on hers and he murmured, "I am sorry." And then, "We will talk more, but now we must return before Black

Hawk becomes suspicious. Around him I must treat you as a slave, but when we are alone we can be ourselves. You will be safe with me. Thunder Raven and his warriors think I have great power, and now that you are with me, no one dares harm you."

Dawn he learned was her name. She was a child of the dawn, born shortly after sunrise one spring morning. It was hard to keep his eyes from wandering off to her under the watchful eyes of Black Hawk. It was an effort to act disinterested, to be cold, distant.

He woke once during the night and heard breathing. It was a comforting sound, a warmth that filled the black cold recesses of the tepee. She had taken the slaves position at this feet. As his eyes became accustomed to the darkness, he could make out her long black hair flowing over her shoulders and waist, her knees drawn up under her for warmth. He reached out for a soft warm sleeping robe and drew it over her.

Later in the day when he was summoned to Thunder Raven's tepee for the daily discussions he was admonished. "You spoil her with a sleeping robe. She is a slave. You beat a slave or they soon take advantage of you."

Black Raven must have spied on them in the early light of morning and reported to Thunder Raven. He could see the cunning scoundrel hurrying off to carry the tale. He'd have to be more careful in the future.

"I'll take Dawn to show her where to find firewood," he told Black Hawk later after his visit with Thunder Raven.

"You needn't take her," Black Hawk admonished. "One of the women will do that for you."

"I'd rather do it myself. She can help gather medicinal herbs as well as firewood." he retorted brusquely, cutting off any further comment.

As they left the village, he glanced back in time to catch Black Hawk hurrying in the direction of Thunder Raven's tepee. "Look! There goes Black Hawk reporting to Thunder Raven," he chuckled.

"What will Thunder Raven do?"

"Probably nothing. Possibly another lecture. I'll tell him I'm teaching you about medicines so you can help me take care of his people."

They crossed the valley, Dawn trailing subserviently behind, and entered the forest at the valley exit. At first the floor of the forest had been picked clean of fallen branches, cones and other litter suitable for cooking fires. But soon they came upon an almost impenetrable tangle of down timber, dead trees toppled by winter winds and heavy snowfall.

White Owl took Dawn's hand in his and strode ahead into the maize. Dawn tried to match his long stride and then drew back.

"Do we need to hurry?"

"Sorry. No."

"What's to prevent us from leaving this terrible place?"

"Sentinels. They are posted throughout this part of the valley. We are probably being watched this very moment."

Her hand tightened on his. "Don't worry," he reassured her. "We'll start gathering wood and they won't bother us."

They snapped dry branches from the down trees, tied them into bundles with leather thongs and stuffed the bundles with pitch pine cones for starting fires.

It didn't take long to put together four bundles. "This is enough," White Owl announced. "Now let's look for medicinal plants."

"I know little of medicine. A poultice for tick fever. A tea."

"Tick fever? See. You know more than I do. That's new to me."

She smiled appreciatively. He liked the way she smiled, her full lips slightly parted, her eyes searching his. "I like being with you," she said, "I feel happiness, for the first time since I was taken prisoner."

"I too. I've felt I'd never again see my family...my brother, my mother, my father, grandmother. Never see Lake Chal Qe Lee...ride its waters in my canoe. But now you..." and he searched for the words, "now that you are here I could live happily."

They took a meandering exploratory walk on the way back along the south wall. They came to an area where the wall was wet, from melting snow fields high above. Here the ground was damp and a leathery leafed plant with pink flowers grew. It was new to White Owl.

"We'll take a few of the leaves, the flowers and roots." He held a flower up to Dawn, "Do you smell the medicinal aroma that rises from it?"

"No, I do not."

"Well, one day someone will come to us whose symptoms do not fit old patterns and we'll know instinctively that this plant will cure the sickness. It's instinct you'll gain with experience. I expect that some day you will become a great medicine woman like my mother, She Who Sees."

XIII

When White Owl was summoned by Thunder Raven the next morning, he wondered if he would be reprimanded for taking Dawn gathering wood and ran a few answers through his mind; he was teaching her about medicinal plants, receptive mind, natural talent, showing a keen interest, to be helpful with a spreading sickness. But apparently all Thunder Raven had in mind was a game of sticks.

Thunder Raven had his sticks in hand when White Owl arrived and motioned for him to sit down. "Let's have a game. I'm feeling lucky today."

"Perhaps I better let him win a game or two," White Owl thought. "Keep his mind off Dawn and me." Thunder Raven laid his five sticks out in front of him, picked up the Master stick, juggled it about behind his back and held out his two huge fists for White Owl to choose which held the Master. He always took first turn and did not lay a bet until he saw how things were going.

White Owl pointed to the right hand. Thunder Raven's thick lips spread in a greedy smile as he revealed an empty right hand, and then he swooped up one of White Owl's sticks. Good form required that he wait with patience and grace for White Owl to present him with the stick, but being a greedy, boorish person he had none of these qualities of character.

With one win to his advantage, he was now ready to place his bet. "My raven fetish necklace against your snowy owl necklace."

Thunder Raven's necklace contained seven black obsidian raven fetishes, emblem of rank among the ravens. If he won the necklace, it would surely create a rift in their relations. On the other hand his necklace contained but one white agate owl fetish. It was given to him by his uncle on his twelfth summer. He cherished it. It conferred power on its bearer. Thunder Raven lusted for it.

They removed their necklaces and placed them on the floor between them. Thunder Raven reached out and gingerly touched the snowy owl fetish. He struggled with his emotions, desire mingled with fear of its power and magic. He withdrew his hand. White Owl said, "First to win five sticks, the winner. Your play."

Thunder Raven thrust his two clenched fists out in front of him. White Owl looked deeply into his eyes. "Right hand," White Owl said. Thunder Raven opened his right hand reluctantly revealing the Master stick.

Thunder Raven's mind moved slowly. He could not mix up the sequence of his plays. And he would often telegraph his moves. His right hand had tightened under White Owl's bold stare. It was now White Owl's turn.

White Owl moved the Master back and forth rapidly in full view of Thunder Raven. His movements were those of a magician, the hands faster than the eye.

"Left hand." Thunder Raven called out confidently, reaching for the Master stick.

White Owl opened his right hand disclosing the Master, stopping Thunder Raven in full reach. An angry frown crossed his forehead. Then he settled back.

Again White Owl flashed the Master back and forth under Thunder Raven's watchful eyes, and again the Master appeared to stop in his left hand.

"Left hand," Thunder Raven bellowed and when the Master appeared in White Owl's opened right hand angrily snatched it away. He turned it over and over.

"Something wrong?" White Owl asked innocently. Score now two to one, White Owl's favor.

"No," Thunder Raven mumbled, returning the Master.

"Care to use your Master?"

"No, no. Go ahead." Thunder Raven replied determinedly, leaning forward, tensely awaiting White Owl's next play.

White Owl rolled the Master around in his right hand, closed the hand, stuck his two fists together and stretched them out.

Thunder Raven pointed decisively at the right hand. White Owl opened it slowly. It was empty. He turned the hand over. It was not there. He looked questioningly at the left hand, opened it. It was not there.

"Ah, it has gone to the spirit world," White Owl intoned, "The spirits of the fetish are angry."

Thunder Raven was awestruck.

White Owl looked heavenward and then in a somber voice proclaimed, "We must comply with the spirits. The fetish must be restored to their rightful places."

Thunder Raven's hands trembled as he replaced his necklace about his neck. White Owl raised his to the heavens and then replaced it around his neck.

"Play another round? No stakes." White Owl offered.

"No," Thunder Raven muttered. "There are other matters we should talk about."

"Other matters?"

"Yes. How old are you? How many summers?"

"Fourteen."

"Fourteen. About what I thought. You should be thinking of taking a mate. My beautiful daughter would make an ideal mate."

She was a plain girl, subdued, typical of a child of a domineering, powerful parent. Certainly not to be compared with Dawn, who was wonderful. Nice. As nice as she was beautiful.

"You hesitate," Thunder Raven growled. "Is there anything wrong with my daughter," he challenged.

"No...no," White Owl hastened to reply. "You have a daughter you can be proud of."

"You will become in time most powerful among the Ravens." Thunder Raven added.

"Your generosity and confidence in me is overwhelming," White Owl replied.

"Then it is settled?"

"There is no time in a medicine man's life for a woman," White Owl said.

"What about Dawn?"

"She is my slave. She does not take my time away from communing with the spirits. She helps gather and prepare medicines. I am training her to assist me in taking care of the sick and aged."

"You think about it. I'm sure you'll figure out how to handle both a wife and a slave." It was more a threat than a suggestion. It grew quiet and he left.

Walking back to his tepee, White Owl thought, "He wants me to take his daughter so he can control me. But it is Dawn I want. Dawn and I have got to get out of here."

XIV

The perfume of fresh cut pine bows filled the tepee when he stepped inside. The floor was swept clean. Gear was hung from leather thongs tied to the lodge poles. Sleeping robes were piled neatly - everything orderly, clean - a far cry from Thunder Raven's quarters.

Dawn turned to him as he entered, turned from the cookfire in the center of the tent where she was adding roots and meat to a simmering pot. Her hair was let down softly framing her face, falling over her shoulders and lit by sunlight filtering down through the aperture at the apex of the tepee. It stirred him deeply, compelling. He reached out...

"Dawn..." he started.

But she broke in, her voice urgent, "The Bitterroot fever has struck! Already six in the village are down!"

"Is that the fever you told me about?"

"Yes. It comes in the spring of the year. Not long after ice out."

"You mentioned a poultice."

"Yes...a tick brings the fever. It gets in the hair and buries itself in the scalp. A special poultice is placed on it. The tick backs out."

"And the sick one recovers?"

"Yes."

"Always?"

"Yes, if treated soon enough."

"Do you know how to prepare the poultice?"

"It is made from the root and leaves of a yellow flower. Ground fine. Mixed with gum of pine and spread on the scalp.

"Can the flower be found around here?"

"Higher up in alpine meadows. Near the crest of the Bitterroots."

"Let's go talk to Thunder Raven."

When they approached Thunder Raven's tent, they heard the sound of a medicine song coming from within. White Owl shook the tanned deerskin draped over the entrance, and immediately Thunder Raven appeared.

"Mountain fever. It's struck the village. Six are down. We need to gather special medicines," Urgency ringing in his announcement.

"It won't be necessary," Thunder Raven replied impatiently. "My daughter, Mourning Bird, has been stricken and our shaman is with her now."

"Medicine songs won't do it," White Owl cut in.

"Medicine songs and sweat baths." Thunder Raven lashed out angrily.

"He mustn't," Dawn broke in concernedly. "Sweat baths will only weaken her. It is tick fever and only a poultice can save her."

"What does she know?" Thunder Raven ranted on.

"She knows what to do. The poultice is a tribal remedy handed down over many generations. We need to go up into the mountains to get fresh medicine roots to make the poultices. We need your approval."

Thunder Raven frowned thoughtfully, finally agreeing to send two warriors with them, "To make sure you get back!"

They searched the high country finally locating a patch of the yellow blossom plant growing along the grassy banks of an alpine meadow. They secured an ample supply of the roots and also gum from pines growing in the vicinity. Upon their return they went directly to Thunder Raven's tepee.

They found him in a black mood. "Where have you been?" he exploded. "Mourning Bird's becoming paralyzed!"

Dawn smiled. "Don't worry," she said softly, comfortingly. "She's going to be alright. Now you and White Owl get outside. Give me room to work."

She turned to find the Shaman staring at her, pouting, belligerent. She smiled, "Won't you sing your medicine songs. They comfort her."

Saved from loss of face by her kindness, he took his rightful place at the side of his patient and raised his voice in song. It was in truth a pleasant voice, modulated and genuinely comforting.

Dawn placed a few shavings from the flower's roots along with some of the leaves and a sprinkling of pine gum in a stone mortar. She ground it to a smooth thin paste with a stone pestal. She located where the tick burrowed into Mourning Bird's scalp and put paste over it. Soon the tick came backing out. She caught it and crushed it under her feet. She rubbed more paste into the wound to draw out any remaining poison.

Dawn patted Mourning Bird's arm reassuringly, "You'll soon feel much better. Now I must go and help the others who are sick. But I'll come back to check on you."

Mourning Bird looked up shyly. Her lips moved weakly. "Thank you..."

Dawn smiled, again patted Mourning Bird's arm and stepped out into the bright sunlight. Thunder Raven strode up to her, concern showing in his eyes, asked humbly, no longer the blustering bully, "Mourning Bird, how is she?"

"Weak, but she will be fine. The tick is out...the paralysis will subside. Now I must take care of the others. Everyone should be warned to check himself for ticks and destroy them."

Thunder Raven nodded and disappeared into his tepee. White Owl fell in with Dawn. "You're not taking their shaman with us?"

"No," she laughed. "They'll get well without him. All that's needed is to get the tick out. He's a comfort to Mourning Bird. She's really quite nice. Shy. Nothing like Thunder Raven."

"Rather plain."

"I put one of the flower blossoms in her hair. She's really quite pretty."

"Oh? I'll have to take another look at her," and he smiled impishly. "Matter of fact, Thunder Raven wants me to marry her."

"What?"

"Thunder Raven wants me to marry her."

She looked up at him flirtatiously through half shut eyelashes, "She would be good for you—being the daughter of a chieftain and all—much prettier than I."

"Heavens no," he rushed to make amends. "You are much more beautiful. I was only teasing you. You know it's you I want."

"No, I didn't," she coaxed.

He laughed. "You are charming..." and thought, you are the most wonderful girl I've ever known.

At the first tepee, word of the miracle cure had already preceded them. They were received as though they were messengers of the gods. They were offered food, delicacies; bitterroot cakes stuffed with dried berries, toasted pine nuts, strips of smoked trout. Then they were escorted to the sleeping furs of the sick one, a child of four or five summers.

Dawn located the tick partly buried in the child's scalp and placed a poultice on it. The child whimpered fearfully. Dawn took her hand in hers and softly hummed her own medicine song to her.

White Owl asked her, "Would you like to see the disappearing stone?"

113

"Yes," she would.

White Owl took a bright red agate from his medicine bag. He held it out to her in his right hand, threw it into the air, caught it, opened his hand and the stone was gone. He reached behind her right ear and produced the stone.

She giggled delightedly, "More."

He put the stone in his mouth, swallowed with difficulty, rubbed his stomach, opened his hand and there was the stone.

"More," she pleaded.

"I must check the poultice," Dawn said gently. "Ah, there it is," and she held the tick in her hand for the little girl to see. Then she dropped it into the cooking fire and it sizzled.

"Now we must see the other sick boys and girls." Dawn ran a hand through the little girl's hair.

"Come back."

"We'll be back," Dawn and White Owl assured her. Then White Owl dug into his medicine bag, pulled out one of the small red agates and gave it to her.

They treated six more tick patients, two adults and four children. The children had played in the woods and were more exposed to the ticks.

They stopped at Thunder Raven's Tepee after the last patient. Mourning Bird was sitting up taking nourishment. She extended a hand to Dawn and smiling drew her down onto a pile of furs beside her. "I feel much better. Thank you. I am sorry for what our warriors did to your people. I hope you and I can be friends."

"I would like that," Dawn replied, her eyes moistening.

A figure blotted out the light at the opening of the tepee and Thunder Raven stepped in. He frowned when he saw someone sitting beside his daughter. Then as his eyes became adjusted to the dim light, a smile broke across his face, the first White Owl had ever seen.

"Ah, Dawn." Thunder Raven said and then, "I see Mourning Bird is better."

"It was nothing," Dawn protested sweetly.

"Many have died in the past. You saved my daughter's life." He seemed tired, emptied of malice. "I want you to learn all you can of medicine from White Owl. You shall become a medicine woman."

He turned from her to White Owl, "Teach her of medicines and healing."

And then he looked at Dawn, "You are no more a slave. You are a daughter of the Ravens."

114

The scene of carnage and wreckage of her village flashed across Dawn's mind, yet she steeled herself to smile demurely for Mourning Bird's sake.

On the way back to the tepee, Dawn said, "Thunder Raven has mellowed."

"Mourning Bird is all he has left," White Owl replied. "His wife and son were killed by the plains Indians. It left scars on his soul."

XV

White Owl was quiet the next morning. It was so unusual, entirely unlike him. He usually woke bright and sunny, talkative as a jaybird. He would bound out of the tepee and off to the stream for his ritual cleansing of body and spirit.

Dawn wondered if it were something she had said or done or could he already be tiring of her? He had such a faraway look in his eyes. Her voice betraying her agitation, she asked, "Is anything wrong?"

"No," he hastened to reassure her. "It's the time of the camas gathering along the ntxwe. We invite neighboring tribes to come visit and dig their winter roots. It's an exciting time."

And then he said, "I wonder if I'll ever see it again."

She saw the frown gather on his forehead and tenderly answered, "You'll see it. Why don't you walk with me to get water? I'd like to hear more about the camas."

She picked up the water pail and stepped out on the trail to the stream. He hurried to join her, grateful to be off and doing something. She walked ahead quickly, stooping once to pick a small pink flower and tucked it into her hair. His eyes fastened on her retreating figure, the grace of her movements, the alluring swing of her hips and shoulders.

At the stream, Dawn knelt on a flat stone and scooped a pail of water. Two small brightly spotted trout that had been hanging in the current at the lip of the pool took flight. Dawn laughed delightedly, "They're so pretty. Did you see them?"

"Yes. They'll wander downstream and grow big one day," he said, the joy of her laughter bringing a smile to his face.

"Now tell me more about the camas," Dawn prompted settling down on a comfortable worn log.

White Owl sat down on the ground beside her, back resting against the log, his right shoulder lightly touching her thigh. "As I said, it's an exciting time. Relatives and friends come from all over."

"I see," she nodded. "Go on."

"It's a festival. Every afternoon there are contests; diving, wrestling, hopping." He warmed to the telling. "Men cast darts with their atlatls at rolling hoops. Women and men play a game with sticks and stuffed leather ball."

"Oh what fun. How exciting," Dawn exclaimed, clapping her hands in delight.

"Yes," White Owl smiled. "But most exciting of all is the stick game played in the evenings between tribal teams. The stick game songs and the clacking of the sticks carry up and down the river."

"Crowds gather around the players. Betting is heavy. Embarrassing amounts of property change hands."

"All you did was play games?" she teased.

"No!" he protested and then laughed. "Actually it's a time you'd like. The valley is so beautiful. The lowlands are abloom with the light lavender flowers of the camas. From a distance it all looks like a great lavender lake."

"It sounds so wonderful. But how do you gather the camas?"

"The gathering is accompanied with ritual. First Great Bear prays to Amot'ken for his blessing. Then he appoints a woman to lead the gatherers."

"When the leader and women reach the camas fields she also prays to Amot'ken. Then, using sticks slightly curved at the point, they pry the camas bulbs loose from the moist ground and put them in cedar hip baskets.

"I think I'd like to try it."

"You'd love it. I'm sure you'd become a leader."

"On the third day," he smiled, "the First Fruits Ceremony is performed. A few camas are cooked and taken to Great Bear. Great Bear calls the men together and they eat the camas. Then all are free to dig as many camas as they will need for…" White Owl stopped and looked questioningly towards the village.

Turning to Dawn he asked, "Do you hear that?"

She put a hand on his arm, "Voices coming from the village?"

"Yes, and it is growing louder. We better see what's going on."

As they broke out into the open, a babble of voices arose from the center of the village. Through the tepees they could see a crowd gathering around a single man who bore a large pack on his back. He turned towards them, stared briefly and then turned away.

Black Hawk appeared and hustled them into the tepee. "Stay inside," he ordered and then casually dropped to his knees beside the opening.

They retreated to the far side of the tepee. "I know him," White Owl whispered in Dawn's ear.

116

"Who?" she asked softly.

"The one with the pack."

"Who is he?"

"Many Pelts. He's a trader."

"Do you think he saw us?"

"He looked this way but he didn't show any recognition."

"How do you know him?"

"He has stopped at our village. But it's been some time since he last visited the No Quosh Kol."

Black Hawk stirred at the opening. His full attention had been riveted on what was going on in the village. He poked his head into the tepee. "I'm going to check on what's going on. Do not leave the tepee!"

They watched Black Hawk make his way through the tepees and up to the gathering crowd. He shouldered his way in. And then he was lost to view as the crowd closed behind him.

They caught glimpses of Many Pelts from time to time as the crowd opened up to let someone out. "They always look excited with whatever they get," Dawn said wistfully.

"He brings exotic things from far places," White Owl exclaimed, "shells, masks, hats, carvings, exotic pelts, flint, gem stones."

"Where will he go from here?"

"Probably to the Flatheads if he hasn't already been there. And then down river to the No Quosh Kols."

"Is there any way we can get word to him?"

"Hardly. He did look long and hard this way, but whether he recognized me or not I can't say. Black Hawk hurried us into the tepee before I could send a message in sign language…"

"Speaking of Black Hawk," Dawn cut in, "here he comes."

White Owl turned quickly and watched as Black Hawk strode arrogantly up to the tepee opening. He threw two rare spotted cat pelts and a large chunk of sky blue stone at Dawn's feet.

"From the lands far below, yours if you will come with me," and then he looked insolently at White Owl challenging.

White Owl rose to his feet, reached out, took hold of Black Hawks' right wrist and drew him tight against his chest. Surprise filled Black Hawk's eyes as he felt the bones in his wrist giving under the pressure. He found himself locked directly into White Owl's cold staring eyes.

"I don't think she's interested," White Owl said quietly. And then he pushed Black Hawk away from him, slowly releasing his arm.

Black Hawk scooped up the pelts and stone, mumbled, "I won't forget this," and slunk out of the tepee.

"What will he do?" Dawn asked, her eyes wide.

"Alone, nothing. But he's devious like sen 'CHAYT le,' the coyote. He must be watched."

Not long after, they saw Mourning Bird leave Thunder Raven's tepee and hurry towards them. She had taken a liking to Dawn and she visited often. But as she neared the tepee they could see she was agitated.

The words tumbled out, "Thunder Raven. He's acting strangely. Can you come?"

"Of course," White Owl assured her. And as he and Dawn walked back with her, asked, "Strangely? How do you mean?"

"He tries to talk but words do not come out. And he can't move his arms or legs."

"Did he see Black Hawk this morning?"

"Yes, Thunder Raven and Black Hawk argued. Black Hawk and the younger warriors want more raids. But Thunder Raven said, 'I am tired. I want no more raids.' Black Hawk shouted, 'You grow old. All you want is to play games. You are too old to lead the Ravens!' Thunder Raven became enraged. He reached for Black Hawk's neck. He stumbled, fell to his knees, then over on his back. His eyes rolled up. He was helpless. Black Hawk stormed out."

Turning to Dawn, White Owl exclaimed, "That explains Black Hawk's actions this morning. It also bodes trouble."

As they came up to the opening of Thunder Raven's tepee. Mourning Bird asked, "White Owl, would you go in first?"

"Of course."

Thunder Raven lay motionless on his sleeping furs, his eyes staring upwards. White Owl reached down and touched his cheek. It was cold. "He's gone to the spirit world," he said quietly, sympathetically, confirming what they already suspected.

Dawn placed a comforting arm around Mourning Bird.

"I can feel no great sorrow." Mourning Bird spoke softly. "He was always good to me but so cruel to others."

"We must move quickly," White Owl said. "First we must get word to the council. Secretly. Black Hawk and the young warriors may attempt a take over."

White Owl looked at Mourning Bird, "The council. Are they to be trusted?"

"Yes, I believe they will be faithful to me," Mourning Bird answered, now heir apparent to Thunder Raven.

"To meet in the council lodge would raise Black Hawk's suspicions. Likewise if we met here. Why not in my tepee. After dark." White Owl offered.

"Yes, I like that," Mourning Bird replied. "I will get word to them."

"Be careful. Wait for dark. Bring Thunder Raven's atlatl and a supply of darts."

White Owl turned to leave, stopped abruptly, "Many Pelts! If we can get word to him."

"It's too late. I saw him packed and leaving on my way over to see you."

XVI

Dusk was settling in the valley when the beat of drums rolled through the village. White Owl looked through the opening of the tepee and saw a large fire on the village commons. Prancing and leaping about it were Black Hawk and his painted warriors, in preparation for a raid.

"Already they rebel," White Owl said. "It's just as well they go tonight. It will give us time to meet with the council."

"Yes, and to do something about Thunder Raven," Dawn put in.

"Thunder Raven. Yes. That's one for the council to decide."

They had just finished eating when the first of the council arrived, Lone Buffalo. He was old. In fact most of the council were old, and White Owl wondered how effective they would be. Thunder Raven had brow beaten most to the point they dared not disagree with him. Anyone who did disappeared.

Mourning Bird soon followed Lone Buffalo. He looked startled when she presented White Owl with Thunder Raven's atlatl and a large supply of darts. But he said nothing. The five remaining council members soon followed one by one.

"Were any of you seen by Black Hawk or his warriors?" Mourning Bird asked.

"I don't think so," Black Cloud offered, the youngest member of the council. "I passed by the bonfire and the dancers could not have seen beyond the bright light from the fire. I heard Black Hawk boast that they were going on a raid in spite of Thunder Raven. That he had grown soft like a woman and too old to lead the People."

"We will have a few days to prepare for their return," Mourning Bird spoke calmly. "First let us take all of their belongings and place them on the trail in the canyon."

"Good, as woman puts a man's belongings outside the tepee when she no longer wants a man. That is good," Lone Buffalo said.

"What about those who have wives?" Black Cloud asked.

"Few have wives," Mourning Bird said smiling. "I suspect most of the wives will be relieved to be rid of them, and those who aren't can go with their belongings."

"We better be ready for Black Hawk when he returns," White Owl said.

Turning to Black Cloud he asked, "How many men are with him?"

"I would say there are around forty."

"And how many fighting men do we have?"

"Thirty. Older, but still capable of fighting." Black Cloud replied.

"Knowing Black Hawk, what will he do?"

"Probably take cover, wait for darkness and then try to slip up on us. He knows the terrain better than anyone."

"If it were me," Lone Buffalo put in, "I'd fall back and after dark climb the rock slides. Take cover and at daybreak roll rocks and rain darts down on the village."

"In any event, what we need is a barricade," White Owl suggested. "A log barricade, shoulder height, across the edge of the village."

"If they attack us after dusk," he continued, "The evening breezes will be coming down off the mountain tops. We can set fire to the dry meadow grasses before us. It will move faster than a man can run. If we are fortunate we'll catch them trying to slip up on us."

Turning to Black Cloud again, he asked, "Can you build a barricade in two days?"

"With every man, woman and child helping, yes, we can do it." Black Cloud replied.

"I like your plan, White Owl," Mourning Bird approved exuding a force and confidence that won the immediate loyalty of the council. "At daybreak start the barricade. There's ample down timber at the blowdown."

"And now, Thunder Raven. We must deal with his remains. Any suggestions?"

White Owl liked the way she sought the thoughts of the council, drawing them into the decision making. It was far different from the browbeating rule by fear methods of Thunder Raven.

Lone Buffalo again spoke first, "Normally we would send him to the world beyond with ancient ritual fitting a chief. But we are faced with a takeover by Black Hawk and his warriors. We should bury him immediately. Later the rites can be performed before all of our people."

"Give me two men, Mourning Bird, and I will do this yet tonight," Black Cloud offered.

"Lone Buffalo, your words are wise," Mourning Bird said respectfully. And then turning to Black Cloud, "I will go with you. White Owl, will you come with us?"

"Yes," White Owl answered, appreciating the confidence she placed in him.

They took Thunder Raven to a grove of whispering trees that bordered the sheer granite wall of the valley. It was a sacred area off from the main stream of village life. They placed Thunder Raven on a rise of ground reserved for chieftains and covered him with stones. It was the time of roses, and on the stones Mourning Bird placed a single rose from the bushes that banked the trail they'd taken in.

Mourning Bird stood quietly looking down then turned and spoke solemnly, without sadness. "It will soon be morning," and then she strode off towards the village.

Shortly after sunrise, the beat of drums rolled through the village summoning everyone to the commons. Beside the sacred circle of firestones stood Mourning Bird, and behind her White Owl and Dawn and the council. She first told the people that Thunder Raven had gone to the world beyond. She spoke quietly, calmly. And then in rising fervor said, "We will no longer live by raiding on our neighbors nor those who drove us off the plains. Our home is here now. It is beautiful, and safe. All captives will be free to return to their people. We shall be hospitable to all. We shall no longer live in fear!"

A murmur of approval ran through the crowd.

"There is no place for Black Hawk and his warriors here," she went on. "We shall put their belongings on the trail by the canyon. By that they shall know they are not wanted. Their wives are welcome here, but those who wish to be with them may leave with them."

"Black Hawk and his warriors have gone on a raid against Thunder Raven's orders. Before leaving, Black Hawk said that Thunder Raven had grown soft like a woman and too old to lead the Ravens. We expect him to attempt a takeover on his return. We are the true Ravens. We shall build a barricade around our village and we shall drive him out. White Owl now bears an atlatl. His power shall be with us. Are you with me?"

A roar of approval rose from the crowd. A chant spread across it in great waves. "Mourning Bird, Mourning Bird, Mourning Bird."

A happy smile broke across Mourning Bird's face and when the crowd quieted she shouted, "Bring a rock, a log, mud. We'll build a barricade strong as the beaver's dam to hold back Black Hawk and his men!"

The crowd broke and scurried about like ants. White Owl drew a semi-circular line on the valley floor anchored on one side to the rock slide and on the other to the granite wall.

They laid on it logs and boulders and cemented them together with mud that soon hardened. By nightfall of the second day the barricade was shoulder high.

XVII

They had been watching since sun-up from the sentinels perch, White Owl, Black Cloud and three other Ravens. Watching the entrance to the valley for the return of Black Hawk, and now the sun was overhead. Heat waves rose from the valley floor, and a dust devil played across the powdery brown dirt. Their mouths were parched, but they dared not slip down to the stream for a drink of cool water.

One moment the entrance to the valley was empty. The next Black Hawk was there standing still, shading his eyes with his upraised right hand, and looking up for the sentinel to wave him and his men on. Then his eyes fastened on the piles beside the trail. He sauntered over to one and realized that a moccasin and a shirt sticking out were his. He dropped his atlatl and pawed wildly through the pile. He stopped suddenly, looked around dumbly for some explanation and then looked up to the sentinel's perch.

White Owl took the moment to step boldly out from the overhang and sweeping his arm towards the canyon shouted, "Take your things and leave! You are no longer wanted among the Ravens." Black Cloud and the others moved into view behind him.

Black Hawk dropped moccasins and shirt and reached for his atlatl. White Owl released a dart from his atlatl tearing the atlatl from Black Hawk's grasp. "Leave now or the next one's for you." White Owl ordered.

Black Hawk broke and scrambled back from the entrance closely followed by his warriors.

It was quiet for some time, and then White Owl caught a movement in the creek bed. Some of Black Hawk's warriors under cover of the bank of the creek were trying to outflank them. A leg was exposed briefly and White Owl put a dart through it. A scream of pain went up followed by a rush of bodies downstream.

"They'll try again at dusk. It's time we go back to the village," White Owl whispered. "When they find we are no longer here, they'll attack the village. We better get ready for them."

There was one weak spot in the barricade where the stream cut through. It was like an open doorway into the village. On his return White Owl placed his major forces on the village side of the stream. The rest he spread out loosely along the length of the barricade.

As the last light faded from the valley, Black Hawk and his men appeared at the far edge. At that distance, they appeared like a black irregular shape. Then three black dots broke from the group and spread out in the waist high dry grass. They moved slowly forward probing for advance guards hidden in the deep grass. They were soon followed by Black Hawk and his warriors. On nearing the village, they sank into the grass, out of sight. The evening breeze that swept down from the mountains stirred the grasses hiding their movement.

White Owl and Black Cloud, armed with torches, leaped over the barricade and set fire to the grass. The night wind fanned it into a raging inferno that swept down the valley fast as a man could run.

Black Hawk and his warriors leaped to their feet, took one startled look back at the oncoming flames. They turned and fled, their arms pumping, their legs outstretched, their fearless leader far out front. Shouts of derision and roar of laughter rose from the on- looking villagers. And then Black Hawk and his men were blotted from view by the towering smoke and flames.

The first light of morning revealed a black, bleak valley. The fire had burned out. It was still. A few wisps of smoke rose from the stark surface. Black blobs showed where those who could not outrace the flames fell.

From behind the barricade, they watched, the three of them, Mourning Bird, Black Cloud, White Owl. The exhilaration of the past night, the high spirits when Black Hawk had been driven off had given way to the reality of daylight. "What a desolate sight," Mourning Bird murmured. "I wonder if it will ever be beautiful again?"

"It will. The rains will come and the grass will grow." White Owl assured her.

"Have we seen the last of Black Hawk?"

"No, I don't think so. We have humiliated him. He will be angry. He'll want revenge. He'll try again."

"Soon?"

"No. They'll hole up, lick their wounds. Dance around a fire. Build up their courage. I expect they'll attack tomorrow at first light."

"What do we do?"

"He has more men than we. Despite their performance today, they are hardened raiders. There will be no grass to cover their attack." White Owl stopped and looked at Black Cloud. "If you were Black Hawk, what would you do?"

"I'd come up the creek bed. Strike where the stream flows through the opening in the barricade."

"Can we block it off with brush?" Mourning Bird asked.

"We could," White Owl said, "But they would spread out along the barricade and attack us at several points. We don't have enough men to cover the whole barricade. Better let them come through the hole. They'll be bunched up. The stream bottom is rocky, slippery, the footing unsure. We can mass our forces there and pour darts into them at short range."

123

"I will leave the fighting up to you," Mourning Bird said, "I'll take the women and children up the exit trail where they'll be safe."

XVIII

"Yes, I am sure it was White Owl," Many Pelts said. After leaving the valley of the Ravens, he had bypassed the Flatheads and the Upper No Quosh Kols and had come directly to the Lower No Quosh Kol. And now he was seated in the council chambers of the Great Lodge with Great Bear, She Who Sees and White Eagle. "I got just a glimpse of him, but he looked exactly like White Eagle. In his hair, he wore a white barred feather, and around his neck a white fetish."

"The body was of someone else, and he has been a captive of these people, the Ravens, all this time?" Great Bear asked.

"Yes. He is closely guarded by a warrior, Black Hawk."

"Where do these people live?" Great Bear asked tensely, rising to his feet.

"In a remote valley surrounded by high cliffs and rocky promontories in the Bitterroot Mountains. The entrance to it is narrow. A few warriors can hold off many. Only a few traders are allowed to enter," Many Pelts replied.

Many Pelt's description fit the dreams of She Who Sees. And for the first time she let herself believe that White Owl truly lived. Her spirits soared and she silently offered a prayer of thanks to Amot'ken.

"Will you take us there?" Great Bear asked.

"There is great danger," Many Pelts replied. "People have gone in and didn't come out."

"Take us there and you shall have a place of honor among the No Quosh Kol, a lodge and a wife of your choosing." Great Bear offered.

A rush of excitement swept over Many Pelts. He had been alone since his tenth summer, his family wiped out by the Ravens. Trading had become a way of life for him. He followed the trade routes, had no ties, was free to go wherever exotic items beckoned.

He roamed from the great plains to the great waters at the edge of the world where the sun disappeared each night. He traded buffalo horns, camas, rare medicinal plants, obsidian from the valley of smokes, soapstone, rare sea shells and magical masks from tribes along the great waters.

He had a sharp traders eye and he was welcomed wherever he went. For him the kindest, most hospitable people were the No Quosh Kol, and their women were the most beautiful. It took but a few moments reflection before he said, "Yes, I shall take you there."

There was feasting and dancing that night honoring Many Pelts. He was rich in exotic wares and he bore the mystery of far off places. The younger women hung on his every word as he told of the exotic sights he'd seen; the leather Mandan Turtles of the east, the shell ornaments and masks of the coastal tribes, the painted desert, the valley of smokes, the lakes where rocks floated. He would be a great catch.

Afterward Great Bear and She Who Sees sat by the sacred fire looking into the embers.

"What do you think of this man?" Great Bear asked, hope tempered with caution. "Can we believe him?"

"He has always been honorable, fair. I have no reason not to believe him." She Who Sees said. "He is one of great power. He learns many things from his travels. I trust him. I will go with you."

"There is great danger. These people are raiders. Their warriors are ruthless. I can't chance taking you."

She Who Sees told Great Bear of her dreams of White Owl and the strange village. "I thought they were just dreams. Now I know they were visions and I saw the village. I feel we should strike soon. Take me with you. I can help."

"Tomorrow I will call the council together. We will speak with them and Many Pelts."

In the council chamber of the Great Lodge, Great Bear met with Many Pelts shortly after daybreak. The eternal fire cast dancing reflections on the pine pole walls. In all his travels, Many Pelts had never seen anything so grand; some forty paces in diameter, the circle of raised logs flattened for the council members to sit on, the dias. It was symbolic of the advanced culture of the No Quosh Kol at the time and most impressive.

Great Bear approached the fire raised two green branches of aromatic pine to the brightness streaming through the aperture above in prayerful supplication to the Guardian Spirits. He then plunged the branches into the fire. They burst into flames and their pungent aroma filled the great room. White smoke rose through the aperture, a signal to the council members to assemble.

The twelve council members soon filed in and took their places. The council was made up of six sub-chiefs and six village elders. She Who Sees was included.

On the raised dias lay a red catlinite pipe. Great Bear lit the pipe with an ember from the sacred fire, pursed his lips, and blew the smoke upwards. He passed the pipe to the elder on his left and each council member in turn repeated the ritual.

Great Bear returned the pipe to the dias. He turned, faced the council resolutely, somberly, and after a long silence spoke. "Many Pelts has brought startling news to us. In a remote village in the Bitterroot Mountains, White Owl is being kept prisoner."

A murmur swept through the council, "White Owl?"

"Yes, White Owl lives," Great Bear said his voice rising. "The body we buried was not his. It was part of a hoax hatched by the Ravens."

Two Cougars, a hot headed sub-chief leaped to his feet and shouted, "War! A war party must be sent to free White Owl and avenge the evil they have done."

Great Bear turned to Many Pelts and spoke quietly, "Let us hear from Many Pelts. He speaks wisely."

Many Pelts rose to his feet. Before he could speak, Two Cougars said harshly, "You are not of the No Quosh Kol. You are from the lands of the morning sun. How do we know you are not one of them?"

"I have no people." Many Pelts spoke calmly, convincingly. "We were once a peaceful tribe like the No Quosh Kol. We were few, our lands bountiful. We lived in peace with our neighbors. Then came the Ravens. The same people who now hold White Owl."

"At night they swept through our village with their warriors killing every man, woman and child, looting. I, a boy of ten summers, alone escaped."

"I am a friend of the No Quosh Kol. Give me twenty of your canoes and sixty of your finest warriors and I will return with White Owl."

Great Bear rose and extending the pipe said, "Let those who agree smoke the pipe." All in turn smoked the sacred pipe.

Many Pelts then said, "I do not trust Black Hawk. We will leave as soon as the canoes can be provisioned."

Great Bear said, "I will go with you. My brother Standing Bear will be in charge while I am gone."

White Eagle said he, too, would go and She Who Sees having waited, listening in the shadows, stepped up and said "I will go, too."

Great Bear turned towards her fully intending to say that a war party was no place for a woman, but then he saw the determined look of her set lips and furrowed brow and smiled broadly.

Shortly thereafter, the war party took off in twenty war canoes. Each carried three warriors. One rested while two paddled. The No Quosh Kol were canoe people. They used them every day of their lives. Given the choice they would rather ride than walk.

The sturgeon nosed canoe was light, fast. Three men taking turns paddling could cover great distances in a short period of time.

Soon they passed the rock ribbed island not far upriver from the village. By the time they reached the 'skaw AY ay,' great elbow in the river, the canoes were beginning to string out. Still in the lead were Great

Bear, She Who Sees, and White Eagle. Driven by concern for White Owl, they set a fast pace for the rest to follow. Close behind was Many Pelts and two sub-chieftains.

Ahead came the muffled sound of falling water, and as they rounded the 'skaw Ay ay,' the great falls of the ntxwe river burst into view. The roar of the falling water was deafening. They beached their canoes on a sandy beach on the south side of the river.

Legend told that coyote, 'sen CHAYT le' the mischief maker, created the falls. A long time ago, he came upriver, seeking a wife. He stopped at No Quosh Kol villages along the way and asked if he might marry one of their beautiful women. When they refused, he became angry and picked up huge stones and threw them into the river making a tremendous splash. The stones created a great waterfall, so high that salmon no longer came up the ntxwe. The No Quosh Kol had to go elsewhere for salmon ever after.

On the north side of the ntxwe sheer granite cliffs rose. On the south side the river banks rose gently. Here at a sandy beach a well worn portage trail took off.

It was an easy portage, short, gentle over most of its length. The canoes were so light, one man could carry a canoe. White Eagle flipped his canoe over and swung it up and onto his shoulders. He took off up the trail at a rapid pace followed closely by Great Bear, and She Who Sees. Many Pelts and the rest came on like a pack of hounds on the scent of a grizzly.

Not far upstream they put in where the water was smooth and deep. They paddled steadily passing several small No Quosh Kol villages, but didn't stop, for word could travel faster than the canoes.

It was dark when they reached the village of the Upper No Quosh Kol located on the banks of the river where it tumbled out of lake ntxwe. They could see the glow of the cooking fires. Again they did not stop but passed by unnoticed on the far side of the river.

The moon came out over the mountains far ahead and lit a trail of sparkling light across the lake. They moved out of the brightness and into the darkness along shore.

Many Pelts paddled abreast of Great Bear and in a low voice said, "Our people are getting tired. We better tie up for the night."

She Who Sees replied, "I have had an ominous feeling today. I fear for White Owl. I suggest we stop for a short rest and then push on."

Great Bear looked at her studying the concern in her eyes and said, "This time we'll follow She Who Sees instincts. We'll put in for a short rest and move on."

At the first sandy beach, the flotilla turned in. They beached the canoes. The warriors straggled off into the woods to relieve themselves and when they returned She Who Sees had spread out dried venison and camas for them to munch on. They sprawled on the still warm sand eating quietly.

The moon had slipped under clouds that had moved in when they returned to the canoes and pulled away from shore. The waters of lake ntxwe lay flat and black.

"We're far enough from the village we can cut directly across the lake. Save some time," Many Pelts said.

"You know the way." Great Bear said. "You lead."

Many Pelts pulled out onto the broad expanse of lake ntxwe. In the distance, the black bulk of mountains loomed on the skyline. To White Eagle they seemed interminably far off. He and Great Bear were now paddling.

Ahead Many Pelts was maintaining a straight line, but White Eagle could see no landmark that Many Pelts was heading for. His arms felt heavy, he was paddling mechanically, pushing to keep pace with Great Bear's rhythmic paddling.

His thoughts drifted off to White Owl. It was the first time since he learned White Owl lived that he'd been able to give thought to him. He wondered how he would look. How had he been treated? Had he been tortured? He thought of Black Hawk. If he'd done anything…the anger boiled up in him. He dug deeper, pulled harder on the paddle, the canoe jumped ahead.

Startled, She Who Sees turned around, "What is it?"

"I was thinking of Black Hawk."

"Forget him," She Who Sees said gently. "Save your strength for when we get there."

Later the moon pulled out from behind the clouds. The mountains changed from black shapeless blobs to ridges and valleys. Ahead a deep valley showed.

Many Pelts turned back and pointed, "The valley of the upper ntxwe river. There is a place to camp at the mouth, but it is on the trade route. We are only a day from the Raven Village. We can't chance word of our presence reaching the Ravens before we do. We'll paddle upriver and camp out of sight."

At first the waters of the river ran smooth and deep through a flat delta. Then as the land rose the river narrowed, picked up speed and alternated between long rapids and deep runs. They came upon a flat topped bench and stopped for the night. They dared not light a fire and again ate dried rations.

At daylight Many Pelts sought out Great Bear. "Tonight we'll be within striking distance of the village of the Ravens. The entrance to the valley will be guarded. High cliffs surround most of the valley. There is a steep narrow cleft in the valley wall behind the village that is guarded by a single sentinel."

"A small force can circle the high cliffs, overcome the sentinel, come down the cleft, rescue White Owl, create a diversion. You could then attack from the front virtually unopposed. I know the country and can lead them there."

"Sounds like a good plan," said Great Bear, "But how will I know when to attack?"

"When you see smoke rising, attack."

White Eagle said to Great Bear, "I want to go with him."

Great Bear read the gleam in his eyes and said, "Many Pelts, take him with you."

Many Pelts nodded and then said, "We'll cache the canoes here and take the trade route. It will be faster."

The trade route was wide, worn smooth by generations of moccasined feet. Many Pelts took the lead setting a tireless loping pace. They were all runners, even She Who Sees, used to covering long distances. It was dark when Many Pelts pulled up. "We're as close to the village as we dare go. They may have sentinels placed from here on in. We'll eat here and rest."

They rested until midnight and then Many Pelts rose and said, "Give me ten men and we'll be off."

"And one woman," She Who Sees said.

"Not this time," Great Bear said determinedly, "It's much too dangerous. I've brought you this far, but from now on you stay out of it. Two warriors will be with you 'til it's over...for your protection."

Many Pelts picked his ten men including White Eagle and set off cross country. They ascended a ridge to their left. It was hand over hand climbing, clutching the shiny leaved buck brush of high country, finally reaching a flat topped mesa. Over to the right was a dark void.

Pointing to it Many Pelts said in a low voice, "Beyond and below lies the valley of the Ravens."

"You've been here before?" White Eagle asked.

"I once crossed over the Bitterroots on the Nez Perce trail and observed the general lay of the land on this side," Many Pelts smiled. "We will circle around to where the cleft in the valley wall is. From now on we must be quiet. Sound carries a long way up here and we must surprise the sentry. He will probably have a small fire."

The forest was open, the ground carpeted in a deep coarse grass. When they reached the cleft there was no fire and no sentry. They searched but no sentry. "Strange," muttered Many Pelts. "There should be one on duty here. White Eagle, we need a scout to go ahead. Give the call of the Owl from time to time so we'll know its clear to follow."

White Eagle nodded his head and entered the cleft. Shortly after Many Pelts and the others followed. A figure broke out of the shadows, and it too entered the cleft.

In the darkness, White Eagle moved slowly downwards, placing each foot carefully, his eyes fastened intently on the trail. He did not see the line of villagers moving upwards toward him. Nor did Mourning Bird see him until at the last moment. She looked up and gasped, "How did you get up here White Owl?"

"I am White Eagle, his brother. And who are you."

"I am Mourning Bird, daughter of Thunder Raven."

By now White Eagle could see there were a number of women and children. "What is going on? Why are you here?"

"Thunder Raven is dead. Black Hawk is trying to take over. He attacked the village and White Owl drove him off by setting fire to the valley grasses. I have brought the women and children here where they will be safe."

A small rock came tumbling down the trail and Many Pelts closely followed by the rest appeared.

"What's this?" Many Pelts asked his brow knit in astonishment.

"I'm not sure," White Eagle replied. "She says she is the daughter of Thunder Raven who is dead and that someone…Black Hawk…is trying to take over the village."

"She is, but what about Black Hawk?" Many Pelts asked.

"We are expecting Black Hawk to attack at first light," Mourning Bird replied. "He has forty battle hardened warriors. We have but thirty - older men. I have brought the women and children here to be safe. White Owl has built a barricade, but he can use your help."

White Eagle looked up at the sky and said, "It won't be long before daylight. We better get down there."

At first glance the village appeared deserted when they arrived. And then they could see figures hunkered down behind the barricade, and over by the stream a concentration of warriors and among them, a head taller than the rest, stood White Owl.

He sensed the intruders and turned seeing Many Pelts, started to say, "Where did you come…and then saw a tall figure, White Eagle. He burst into a smile and they rushed together clasping each other by the shoulders. "White Eagle." "White Owl" they shouted.

They looked long at each other and then White Owl said, "You're just in time. We will soon be under attack. We…"

"That's what Mourning Bird told us," White Eagle put in and then added, "Great Bear and She Who Sees are here, too."

White Owl looked about for them, "Where are they?"

"Back at the entrance to the valley with fifty of our finest warriors. I was to send up a smoke signal when we had rescued you; then create a diversion tying Thunder Raven down here. Great Bear could then attack from the front virtually unopposed."

"Great plan, but if we send up a smoke signal now they'll be pinned down by Black Hawk as they come out of the canyon." Many Pelts put in.

"So, what we do now is build a fire. Then the instant we see Black Hawk we throw green bows on it," White Owl said.

"Yes, a big fire and enough green pine bows to send up a column of smoke that can be seen by Great Bear." Many Pelts added. "Timing will be important."

They built a huge fire midway of the barricade, the leaping flames lighted a wide semi-circle that cut into the night. Nearby they piled freshly cut pine bows.

White Eagle and White Owl were sitting on their heals by the fire when She Who Sees stepped out of the shadows and into the firelight. They were talking animatedly, bringing each other up to date about events of the past year. They didn't notice her at first, then felt her eyes upon them and turned around. They jumped to their feet and asked as one, "What are you doing here!"

"I came to help with the wounded when the fighting starts." She didn't add she could wait no longer to see if White Owl was alright.

White Owl came over and put an arm around her. "I'm glad you came. It's been a long time." How much older she looks, he thought. He's grown to be a man, she thought.

"How did you lose your two guards?" White Eagle smiled.

"They were nice. They looked the other way when I bathed," she giggled.

"Sees, did you notice the tepee among the whispering trees?" White Owl asked.

"Yes?"

"Dawn is there. You'll be safer with her. We'll bring any wounded over there."

"Dawn?"

"My friend. She's wonderful. You'll like her."

Wonderful? She smiled. That sounds serious.

The sky over the mountains to the east was starting to lighten. White Owl and White Eagle and Many Pelts had been watching the far edge of the meadow. The canyon mouth lay darker than the surrounding ridges.

Suddenly shadowy figures, small at that distance, skittered out of the blackness and into the cover along the streambed.

"Throw the green branches on the fire," White Owl shouted. The branches crackled, blazed up briefly and a column of white smoke rose straight up in the still air.

Many Pelts pointed, "He's divided his forces. There on the rock slide to our left...five of his warriors, scrambling over the boulders. If they get above us they can shower us with darts. Give me two men and I'll hold them off."

"Don't go any higher than atlatl range, and you can give us support, too," and White Owl turned to White Eagle, "Spread the rest of your men along the barricade. I'll join my men."

White Owl spread his men in a semi-circle back from the opening in the barricade. There they could pour a withering crossfire as Black Hawk and his men came through. They sank out of sight behind a boulder, a bush, a tree, anything that would hide them momentarily when Black Hawk and his men broke through.

It was quiet. A sentinel watched, but he did not see Black Hawk and his practiced raiders squirming up on their bellies; a weed, a small bush held in front covering their movements.

A battle cry broke out on the rock slide. White Owl looked up to see Black Hawk's men descending the rock slide. One went down from an atlatl dart. And then they were spreading out, out-flanking Many Pelts.

At the same moment howling figures, their faces hideously painted, burst through the opening in the barricade. White Owl and his men rose showering them with darts. It became a milling, hand to hand confusing mass. And then White Owl realized the wiley Black Hawk had again divided his forces. He and his main force had spread out along the barricade.

He shouted to his men, "Follow me," and dashed down the barricade to support White Eagle. Black Hawk now stood on top waving his men over.

It was a devastating moment. Many Pelts was pinned down on the rock slide. Back at the stream some of his men were locked in hand to hand fighting. Black Hawk's best warriors were swarming over the barricade stark against the light of the fire and embers rising in the sky.

The next moment Black Hawk was reaching to the sky, then pitching forward off the wall, a dart sticking out his back. And then as one, Great Bear and his warriors were pouring over the barricade.

Another moment and it had become quiet, dream like. The last you could see was Great Bear, White Eagle and White Owl, as if in slow motion, making their way over to the tepee to She Who Sees and Dawn, and beyond,

Mourning Bird and her people, coming down the trail, returning to their village.

BIBLIOGRAPHY

Carriker, Robert C. The Kalispel People, Phoenix: Indian Tribal
    Series.
Cotes, O.J.,ed. The Kalispels: People of the Pend Oreille. Usk,
    Wash. Kalispel Tribe, l980, with a grant from the Washington
    Commission on the Humanities. Printed at Brigham City,
    Utah by the Office of Technical Assistance and Training
De Smet, Rev. Peter John, S.J. Narrative of a Year's Residence
    Among the Indian Tribes of the Rocky Mountains, l845-46,
    New York: Edward Dunigan, l847.
Diomedi, Alexander, S.J. Sketches of Indian Life, Aquinas
    College Library, Grand Rapids, MI Woodstock: Woodstock
    Press l884.
Fahey, John. The Kalispel Indians, Norman: Universityof
    Oklahoma Press, 1974.
Teit, James A. Salishan Tribes of the Western Plateau, Bureau
    of American Ethnology, l927-28.

ABOUT THE AUTHOR

Tom Lacy is eighty some, well past the years for writing stories. But Masselow is his inspiration, and if he, too, can make it to 94 perhaps he may have another story or two in him. He loves to write. Miss Collette, professor of English at the University of Idaho, was shocked when he told her he would not major in English, but rather in Forestry. He had to get that out of his system, and then spent his career heading up his own ad agency where he honed his skills in creative writing, exaggeration, and prevarication. Majie Failey writes in her latest book, *The Sweeter the Onion*, that, "His humor, his sense of values that comes with being one with nature, and his beautiful gift of description makes his writing sheer delight."